AND PUT AWAY CHILDISH THINGS

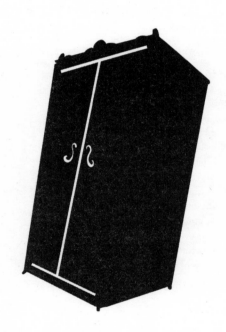

ADRIAN TCHAIKOVSKY

SOLARIS

First published 2023 by Solaris
an imprint of Rebellion Publishing Ltd,
Riverside House, Osney Mead,
Oxford, OX2 0ES, UK

www.solarisbooks.com

ISBN: 978-1-78618-879-3

This book is a work of fiction. Names, characters, places
and incidents are products of the author's imagination or
are used fictitiously.

10 9 8 7 6 5 4 3 2 1

A CIP catalogue record for this book is available from
the British Library.

Designed & typeset by Rebellion Publishing

Printed in the UK

AND
PUT AWAY
CHILDISH
THINGS

It is said that, long ago, there were many ways into the land of Underhill, but one by one they fell away. Until, search as you would, you might never find your way from the comforting world we all know into that place of magic and adventure. But for James and Jemima, fleeing from the cruel Mr Ragstaff, the entrance was just a path into the woods they had never noticed before, twisting between the gnarled old trees...

The Road to Underhill (1947),
Mary Bodie, Golden Century Press

CHAPTER ONE

BREAKING INTO TELEVISION was proving unexpectedly stressful for Harry. Which seemed particularly unfair given that he was on the cusp of forty and had been working in TV for two and a half decades. He'd assumed he'd be in his stride by now, but then he'd made the mistake of swerving out of his lane and suddenly it was this invisible maze of attitude and prejudices, all of which seemed to be personified in Margot Lorne, the semi-beloved presenter of *How Even Me?*

Margot Lorne was not even slightly beloved of, or by, Harry. Their few days of association had kindled an intense, unspoken dislike between the two of them. By mutual and instant agreement they expressed this by being over-jolly and backslappish, all not-quite-touching hugs and kissing the air past their cheeks, each ringing with distaste for their opposite number.

Margot Lorne had gone to a mid-ranking drama school and landed some roles in *The Bill* and *Casualty*. She'd now found her comfortable rut being the pleasant, chatty face of programmes where celebrities got to bare their hearts—usually when they had a book out or a new show on or some other reason to remind the general public of their existence.

Felix 'Harry' Bodie, on the other hand, had gone to a different mid-ranking drama school and scored a couple of roles on *Eastenders* and the early run of *Doctors*. He'd found his feet presenting children's programming as one of the revolving cast of hosts on the CBeebies circuit, providing filler segments between the gaily-coloured puppets and cartoon characters.

They had never even met, before Harry's stint on Margot's program. Possibly the problem was that, right then, Harry had a huge chip on his shoulder about anyone whose broadcasting career *didn't* involve having to work with bloody kids. He had already alienated a fair number of his regular co-hosts for exactly the same reason, because they all seemed to be able to caper and gurn and get through the interminable clapping songs without wanting to drop an F-bomb in front of half a million four-to-seven year olds. Not so he.

And there was the elephant in the room, of course. His other, ersatz claim to fame, that he simultaneously insisted wasn't important while being secretly resentful that it *hadn't* somehow propelled him magically to greater heights of success. The books. Bloody *Underhill*.

And so, because he was in the midst of one of his sporadic

attempts to break into serious drama, he'd agreed to go on *How Even Me?* and expose his genealogy to the glaring public spotlight that was Margot Lorne's warm smile and gentle Scots accent. His agent reckoned it would be good PR at just the time when Harry's resumé turned up on people's desks. And Margot's production company had taken him on because his genealogy included one children's author who was at least vaguely remembered seventy years after her works first came out.

From Margot's perspective, they were doing Harry a solid. From Harry's perspective he was slumming it for the sake of a future career where he didn't have to gurn or caper even a little, save in service of the serious actor's art. By halfway through the first day of filming, taking a chainsaw to the lesser branches of Harry's family tree, they loathed each other with a polite and icy passion.

It turned out that Harry's maternal great-grandfather—hitherto known to the family as a respected captain of industry and Conservative MP hopeful—had been neck-deep in a stock market scandal and had actually done time At Her Majesty's Pleasure. This was unaccountably something that had never come up at the family dinner table, and Margot's expression of woeful sympathy had glimmered with gloating triumph. Harry spent that evening on the phone to the production company, insisting that they cut or downplay it. Hide it amongst the... except they had turned up very little else of interest in that part of the family, so the whole white collar crime angle was looking mighty attractive as a crowd-pleaser.

"It'll be fine," he told a succession of executives, in tones between a grovel and a growl. "We're doing the book stuff tomorrow. Magda—*Mary*—Bodie, my sainted gran. Bury it behind that. And maybe, just maybe, it'll be better than you imagine. You just wait."

Because Gran'd had a secret.

Alright, not a *secret*, because she'd told it to her sole daughter, Harry's mum. She'd told it to Harry. She'd told it to quite a lot of people at the care home and a number of medical professionals, too, but that last, drawn-out part of her life wasn't the way Harry wanted to remember her. A non-secret, then. A non-secret about her own mother, the great-grandmother neither Harry nor anyone else in the family had ever met. The mysterious woman whose stories, back in Magda's own childhood, had been the inspiration for the *Underhill* books in the first place.

"Your great-grandma," she used to say, "was someone very special. She came to this country from somewhere where she was very important." And she'd touch her brow in a special way, and child Harry could almost see the glint of gold and gems there.

And Magda had something of a Slavic feel to it, obviously. And 'Bodie' wasn't necessarily their original surname. And, well, Harry wasn't actually *saying* that he was the rightful Tsar of all the Russias, but he had wondered… Not enough to actually put the legwork into investigating, admittedly, but why would he need to, when he had the whole research team of *How Even Me?* to do it for him? Even if that team was mostly a harassed-looking office junior called Mei.

Which unfortunate piece of nomenclature led to endless 'How even Mei?' jokes from the rest of the crew. Mei was the only person on set who disliked every other human being involved even more than Harry.

Ever the consummate professional, Margot's greeting on the second day was an actor's masterclass in 'How to sparkle for the camera while showing your colleague just how much you dislike him.' At least today they were dealing with the good stuff. In their hearty air-kissing was the understanding that they would both mine today for whatever they could get out of it and then never have to see one another again.

They were in the Oxford Story Museum for the shooting. *How Even Me?* preferred to film in the attics of their guests' grand houses where they could pretend to unearth dusty old photographs of sainted ancestors undergoing privation or doing praiseworthy things. Harry's two-room flat was unaccountably missing an attic, because the house had gone with Lisa—along with most of the money—during the divorce. However, the museum still had a wall panel about the *Underhill* books as one of its permanent exhibits, and probably the whole thing got waved through as mutual good PR that didn't have to impact on anyone's balance sheet too much.

They positioned him in front of the display. There were a couple of first editions, the once-bright covers faded, plus some stills from that 1973 animation and a creepy little puppet from the Polish stop-motion of '87 which still figured in Harry's nightmares. With that as a backdrop, they did the preliminaries, the little interview sections where he reminisced fondly about Granny Magda, or Mary as her pen name had been. He even went so far as to mention *the secret*, those little hints she'd dropped about the provenance of her own mother. And he wasn't really expecting Margot to play God Save the Tsar and then crown him, but it was nice to have the whiff of it hanging in the air. And he relaxed and let his guard down, and then they brought out the box.

"Harry," Margot said. And he'd wanted them to call him Felix. He wanted to start calling himself Felix, instead of the godawful clownish *Harry*, that non-name he'd taken on and which he was thoroughly sick of. But he was Harry Bodie to the world, and to Equity, and his agent reckoned it was still more help than harm when it came to names to conjure with. "Harry," Margot said, "what would you say if I told you that we'd been able to track down some real information about your great-grandmother. Far more than Mary ever told you?"

And, the bitch, she was doing her excited voice, as she did in every show where the guest's past held a cornucopia of riches rather than hardship and grief. And he should have thought that they could easily re-shoot her part later, if she wanted to give it the opposite spin. That the Margot Lorne speaking to him then and there needn't be the one who made it to screen. He fell for it hook, line and sinker.

And they had a box there, an old metal chest that eagle-eyed afficionados of *How Even Me?* might have recognised as turning up in a number of mid-list celebrity attics, because the show got sloppy with re-using its props.

Because they wanted the true and honest reaction, they passed it into his hungry hands for him to open. They'd arranged the papers inside quite carefully, so that their narrative was laid out step by step. The admission notice, the treatment reports, the doctor's notes, the birth certificate. Filming as Harry's excited sounds of discovery ground down to something bleak and sad.

The London County Asylum was stamped on half the pages. That was where his great-grandmother had turned up, apparently. January 8th 1916, which he reckoned was a time when the asylums were doing a booming trade, so small wonder the paperwork looked rushed. Admission of a pregnant woman answering to the name of Devaty Svoboda, initially speaking no English, though she appeared to have picked it up quickly enough. No clue as to where she'd come from, but the country had a lot on its mind right then. And *incurably deranged,* as the spiky handwriting of one professional had it. Possessed of such detailed and elaborate delusions that the specialist had insisted she be kept in residence for study.

She claimed to be the Queen of Fairyland, said the notes.

Her daughter had been taken from her, obviously. Named Magda, at her insistence. Permitted to visit by the unusually lenient foster family, and the indulgent alienist who'd sat in on their encounters. Listened to the increasingly lurid fantasies she'd spun for the kid. Honestly, for a destitute pregnant woman beset by incurable delusions, great-granma had fallen on her feet. She'd died in the institution in 1930, the records said, of pneumonia.

And Harry did his best, and probably he could have turned the whole thing into a career exercise whereby he used the heartstrings of the audience as bootstraps for his upcoming career. But in that instant, wrong-footed as he was, he was just so painfully aware that Margot Lorne and her entire crew were laughing at him. That they'd all taken a profound dislike to him from the first moment he turned up, on the not-unreasonable basis that he had made himself profoundly dislikeable. And so his reaction was less noble sorrow and more peevish anger that his goddamn great-grandmother hadn't been anything more useful to him, and the cameras were rolling all the time.

Worse than that, if even possible, was the next two months of him calling the production company with threats, and then having his agent call them with the same threats phrased in more professionally appropriate language, and then having some lawyers call them with different threats that cost Harry rather more money than he'd have preferred to spend and got him precisely nowhere. He'd signed a contract before going on the show and nowhere in that contract did the words 'power of veto' appear, and so they were damn well going to use what they'd got. And at last, just as he was doing his bit in the CBeebies 2019 Christmas panto, the show was broadcast and it all became public knowledge.

Enough interest was generated by the clashing wheels of 'Children's TV presenter' and 'madness in the family' for him to become a cause célèbre in the worst way. A little digging by responsible journalists turned up his own string of therapists, and the failed marriage, and the couple of years when his drinking had got seriously out of hand. It hadn't taken a great deal of glue to stick these together into the picture of a man with his own issues, inherited or otherwise. And then, given that it was the start of 2020 and people were beginning to get twitchy about this new virus, the news cycle moved on.

His agent, Steve, was pessimistic over the phone. "I hate to say it, but... it's the queen of fairyland bit. People are funny about mental health, aren't they? Doesn't exactly jibe with 'serious proper actor.' Unless you fancy milking it?"

Play up the sorrow and the woe about poor great-granma. Ostentatiously do a charity gig for an appropriately themed good cause. The sort of thing that Felix 'Harry' Bodie, hungry would-be grown-up actor, would do. Except Harry had, by then, watched his own lamentable performance on *How Even Me?* approximately nine thousand times and had come to the conclusion that Felix 'Harry' Bodie was a bit of a shit, and that his great-grandmother had genuinely been hard done by. He discovered, to his surprise, that he didn't have the heart to turn his family sorrows into a career mill after all. The thought of the bedridden old woman insisting she was Queen of Nowhere to the daughter she hadn't been able to keep... It turned out there were actually depths he wasn't willing to plumb.

"Felix, mate, you're not exactly helping me here," said Steve, and Felix said rather sharply that he'd thought it was the *agent's* job to help *him*, and that was another bridge half-burned.

And there were looks from his colleagues at the BBC, and on the street as well. When the occasional kid wanted a photo, he could read any kind of pity or lip-curling disdain he wanted into the expressions of the adults. It was as though a brush had reached out a century through time and tarred him with mental instability. *He's the one with the madwoman in his family. Is he dangerous, do you think? Should he even be as close to our children as on the other side of the TV screen?*

He started drinking again. Or drinking *more*, because despite all the professional advice he'd never been able to go dry. Not in entertainment, where everyone was positively pickling themselves the moment they turned the cameras off. He was definitely drunk when he came back to his flat in the small hours one night in February, after the world had mostly forgotten about him again. He was drunk when he dropped his keys in the rosebush-snarled patch of garden out front and ended up on his hands and knees, muttering to himself as he tried to find them. It hadn't been a good night. The pub had been mostly empty, his fellow TV types crying off because of the growing aversion to crowds and public spaces. He'd downed four solitary pints and then swung by the off licence so he could take the festivities home with him. He felt he was watching his career and life fall apart in slow motion, and every time he had a chance to reverse the course, somehow he did exactly the opposite. Which left him cursing God, the Devil and several named production executives as he fumbled for his lost keys in the near pitch dark and skewered himself on rose thorns.

"Here," said someone, and abruptly the missing items were dangling before his face. He staggered upright, snatching them from the air on the second try, feeling their inarguable cold metal edges pressing into his palm. Crusted with soil from the garden, as though they'd been unearthed from a grave.

"What? Right. Thanks," he blurted out and then looked at the someone and sobered up pretty much immediately.

Not literally, of course, biochemistry working as it does, but a savage cocktail of other hormones overrode the worst of the drink because something in him was screaming *fight or flight!* and, being a sedentary middle-aged TV presenter, he just froze up and did neither.

Tall. Freakishly tall. Although as Harry was only five foot eight maybe just 'very tall.' Wearing a long coat, like a flasher. Standing weirdly, every part of him held wrong. The legs as though the man was right on the balls of his feet, and then those feet were stretched too long. Sour reek of spoilt milk. Aquiline face with a briar-patch beard and sunken eyes. Filthy, ancient, like a vagrant. Like an icon of a saint unearthed from a dig site. Looked at one way, exactly the sort of disturbed homeless man Harry would cross the street to avoid. Looked at another, an ancient king.

The horns. They were ridged like a ram's, curving back into rook's nest hair. The roots of them, growing from his temples, were unmissable.

"Harry Bodie," said the thing. Said the *delusion,* incipient madness, drink-born hallucination. And "No!" shrieked Harry Bodie, dashing for the door. Fumbling the newly reclaimed keys in the lock, waiting for the long, bony hand on his shoulder. Slamming the door behind him loud enough to wake everyone in the building. Trying the door three times to reassure himself it had locked. Not looking out there. Not glancing back as he thundered up the stairs. Not giving himself a moment's thought. And the window of his flat only faced an alley, and he didn't look out of it anyway.

And when he awoke the next morning, hungover and still dressed, none of it had gone away. None of it had proved soluble in the alcohol he'd imbibed that night. There had been a man with horns and goat legs in the garden and, because there patently couldn't have been a man with horns and goat legs in the garden, that meant he must be going mad.

"But where is my medal?" Wish Dog howled. "Without it I cannot call my friends, and without them the ogre will run all the way to the castle gates!"

"It is that rascal Timon," Jemima cried out. "He has taken it for his coat."

James nodded. "Then you must find where he is hiding and claim it back, and Wish Dog and I will slow the ogre as best we can while you do."

Now, while the children were saying this, Timon the Faun was running helter-skelter through the Maldry Woods. At first he had been running because he wanted to bring the medal home as swiftly as possible. Then he had been running because he had thought how angry Wish Dog might be. At last, he was running even faster because the Maldry Woods were not a friendly place and he was being chased. Following his hoofprints, patient and dreadful, came the long-legged stride of...

The Giants of Underhill (1949),
Mary Bodie, Golden Century Press

CHAPTER TWO

THE *UNDERHILL* BOOKS were still in print, and indeed a slow trickle of royalties made a sporadic contribution to Harry's rent via the fund that oversaw the estate. They were the usual sort of post-war kids' stuff, born out of a world of rationing so that the young protagonists' rewards for fighting giants or recovering stolen jewellery was often no more than a decent meal, which they were glad to get. They were '50s nostalgia that the Baby Boom generation had grown up on, about another world that was green and magical and *nice* and constantly under threat by monsters both buffoonish and genuinely monstrous. And there had been a magic dog and a tree spirit woman. And a Hilarious Clown which, even just in print on the page, had creeped young Felix the fuck out, frankly.

And a faun.

And the faun in the books, about whom the adjective 'rascally' was used rather more often than necessary, had not much resembled the figure he had seen in the garden. There had been no rascalhood about that ancient-mariner apparition. Two days after the event, the sight was still knife-edge sharp in his mind. He kept waiting for time to blur it to a point where he could discount the whole business and move on. It didn't happen. The sight of the horned destitute was imprinted on his mind as hard as if the man had headbutted him.

It wasn't as though the old demons of anxiety and depression were being kept far from the door, what with the *How Even Me?* fallout. And he'd had the odd hallucination before. Real enough in the moment, far more easily dismissed in retrospect. And therapists had put them down to stress or, in one case, some spectacular side-effects of mis-prescribed medication. It wouldn't even be the first time he'd hallucinated something that might plausibly be connected with the whole *Underhill* nonsense, which had been on his mind recently, for obvious reasons.

Another thing he did, as well as get anxious and depressed and see things, was what one specialist had called 'unhealthy ideation.' Not even about himself, per se, but taking ideas into grotesque places that he couldn't then un-think. He'd made the mistake of telling his agent about it once, and Steve had said, "Harry, mate, write it down. Do me a script. This stuff's gold dust right now." And hadn't understood why Harry would rather have pulled his own fingernails out than make it any more *real*.

"It'll be, what's the word, an exorcism, mate. Catharsis, isn't it."

Harry was very worried that it wouldn't be at all cathartic; less an exorcism than a conjuration. And again, that had been him not being *helpful*.

When he had been very young, and an avid reader of his own gran's books, he had wished that the various colourful characters would actually turn up in his life. That he could play games with the dog and the faun. Although not with Gombles the Clown, that godawful nightmare who Gran obviously felt was such a fucking *riot*. And now, forty years old, his 'unhealthy ideation' presented him with a gleefully detailed scenario to add to the list of things he couldn't un-see. *What if you got your wish back then?* his mind whispered to him in the small hours, impervious to the scotch he'd knocked back. *Except what if they just couldn't find you? What if they've been searching all these years, getting old, getting angry, and now they've finally turned up to play...*

"Fuck off!" he shouted at the top of his voice at three in the morning, because insomnia was in the mix as well. The residents in the neighbouring flats likely didn't appreciate that he meant his inner demons and not them.

Work was problematic, what with the new precautions and restrictions they were bringing in, and which Harry was too tired and, sometimes, hungover to get his head round. And he couldn't exactly say, 'Well, yes, but I saw an impossible monster-man in the garden last week so I'm still a bit fragile,' because that would only make things worse.

Mid-February brought a suspicious absence from someone on the crew, rumours of serious illness, and then Harry ended up pre-recording a great undigested wodge of links and getting sent home along with most of his little clique of presenters. *Await further instructions*, went the instructions, which were not then followed by any further instructions.

Too much time on Harry's hands brought fragmentary nights broken up by a shotgun pattern of waking out of bad dreams. In those dreams, his unhealthy ideation was having a field day, and it wasn't just the *Underhill* characters who'd been making their way for decades in an unfriendly human world. It was all the comic cartoon creations from the kids' shows he'd done linking segments for. The Claymation penguins and anthropomorphic vegetables and glove-puppet caterpillars. All of them grown up and eking out a living as supermarket checkout clerks and office cleaners; as accountants and secretaries and technical helpline call centre telephonists. Trying to work out how to pay their taxes when their arms were moved by rods and they had no opposable digits. Explaining to the police how they'd swerved and knocked out the driver's side headlamp of a bus when they were a 2D scribble of a freckled girl with unfeasibly long pigtails, or a Picassoan cartoon pig with both eyes on the same side of its face. And the real-world human policeman would nod and frown and make notes, and the cartoon pig or duck or flower would be getting more and more anxious as they tried to explain that they were late for work now, and there were bills to pay, and it was a long time since they'd been on that programme or in that happy little book about friendship. And couldn't the policeman just cut them some slack, because their cartoon moose spouse was already talking about going to their cartoon moose parents to get some space to think about the marriage, and little Timmy the moose-duck-flower-pig-whatever was getting teased at school, probably for being some sort of cartoon hideous monster-animal-plant hybrid as far as Harry was concerned, and, and...

And he woke up in tears at the desperate, doomed attempts of all the kids' TV characters to navigate the banal complexities of the world, as they lost their credit cards and got the wrong times for meetings and were hopelessly baffled by Microsoft PowerPoint so that the big presentation for work on Monday was an unmitigated disaster. And the dreams weren't even about *him*. He was just a powerless observer watching these stupid cartoon animals ruin their lives.

As though all of this really *had* been some kind of exorcism, his agent got on the phone the next day to say that Birmingham Rep had made some enquiries about whether he might be Edgar in a production of *Lear* they were looking at. And he bit back a lot of bile about this just being because they wanted to capitalise on his family history of lunacy, and said yes, that would be lovely, serious acting role, just the thing. Because it was a good part, and it was a good company, and who really *cared* what ulterior motives there might be behind the casting?

When a call came through soon after, he thought it was probably someone from the Rep, and answered it immediately. And then there was a bit of a pause on the other end and he went very cold and scared—and somehow unable to kill the call—in case the voice that eventually came to him should be that of an ancient destitute faun. He couldn't even have said what that would *sound* like. He just knew he'd recognise it.

The voice that finally spoke was a woman's, though, and there was nothing particularly decaying or faun-like about it. Dry, a smoker's roughness overlaying faded posh. The sort of voice he knew from actors who'd had some family cash backing them a while back but had been making their own way since. Not unlike his own, he supposed.

"Is that Mr Bodie?" she asked, and he realised the long pause preceding that might have been because he hadn't said anything when he answered the call. And then: "Mr Felix Bodie?" And, of course, he was Harry to just about anyone in the business, and Harold to spam callers because of the way he filled in internet forms. Being addressed by his actual name was the only thing that stopped him putting the phone down.

"Who is this?" he asked. "I mean, yes, it is. Are you the press?" Simultaneously feeling the plunge of *Are they not done with me?* and the swoop of *Perhaps they're not done with me?*

"My name's Rebecca Seitchman, Mr Bodie. I'm calling from Seitchman and Sachs, solicitors."

Jesus, what now? What had he done to have the relentless hounds of litigation set on him?

"Mr Bodie?"

"What's this about?" Hearing his voice shake. "Look, aren't you supposed to send me a letter? My agent usually fields them—or can I give you my lawyer's details?" Although that would involve him having to *pay* his lawyers.

"Ah, no," Seitchman said, after a moment. "This isn't one of *those* calls." She sounded as though she was enjoying herself, which he felt was a terrifying trait in a solicitor. "Actually, I wanted to talk to you about a potential claim you might be in a position to bring—"

"Oh, Jesus, no, you are not going to start talking about—look, I never took out any PPP. I don't even know what it stands for. I wasn't in a car accident. I don't own a car. I haven't—"

"Mr Bodie, it's about the Underhill IP."

For a moment he heard *Underhill IPA* and wondered if the trust had licensed a children's book series to a brewery. While it didn't seem likely, he'd seen a faun in the garden and so wasn't the best arbiter of plausibility. Then his brain caught up. Intellectual Property. Lawyer stuff.

"The trust handles—" he said weakly, but she cut him off.

"Mr Bodie, I just happened to be researching one of my regular cases when I came across some information relating to the Underhill books and your family. And you'd been on, you know, *that* program recently, so you were on my mind. It struck me that there might be an opportunity associated with it, that would devolve to *you*, as the direct heir of Magda Bodie."

This was all sounding ninety per cent like a personally tailored scam, and doubtless Seitchman would be asking for his bank details any moment. On the other hand, the remaining ten per cent was made of the ephemeral dream of free money and Harry kept trying to kill the call and never quite made it.

"Go on."

"Mr Bodie, I think that we should meet," Seitchman said. "I'd like to show you some documents, and I don't want to send scans or anything by email. It's a matter that would benefit both from quick action and from playing our cards close to our chest. Once we've met and talked, and I've explained to you the full situation, you can make the call on whether you want to proceed."

None of this sounded remotely legit. But then if a solicitor couldn't solicit, then where would the world be? "Where are your offices?" he asked, aware that he was being suckered into something.

"I'll come to you," Seitchman said briskly. "Or near to you. You know the Bombay Sapphire on Kent Street?"

"I—er, yes...?" It was a decent Tandoori in the little knot of shops and bars a short bus-ride, or long walk, from the flat. It was not a traditional site of clandestine meetings with mystery lawyers, to the best of Harry's knowledge.

"Tonight, nine o'clock, suit you?"

"I—er, yes...?" Feeling helplessly carried along by the current of the conversation.

"Excellent. See you then."

He wasn't going to go. Everything about the conversation had been wrong, start to finish. Respectable lawyers didn't just call up out of the blue trying to interest you in an intellectual property claim. They didn't want to meet you at your local Indian restaurant. It was all patently nonsense. He should stay home and read *King Lear* instead, in case the Birmingham Rep thing came through. *This cold night will turn us all to fools and madmen*, he decided.

Nope. Not doing it. Not a chance in hell.

He arrived at the Sapphire at eight thirty, because if he *was* doing this stupid thing then he might as well do it in a particularly clever and/or even more stupid way. He was going to not actually turn up at nine, because he'd already be in a position to watch the Sapphire and see who was going in and out, and maybe pick out who this Seitchman was. He ensconced himself at a table by the window of the burger bar across the street and munched fries while he watched the Sapphire's door like a hawk.

His search criteria were predicated on Seitchman being alone, a woman, and dressed at least reasonably professionally. Probably carrying a briefcase, if there were documents involved. As it was, the Sapphire's few visitors were mostly getting take-out. The little high street was like a film set where they'd run out of budget to hire extras. He saw a few office lads just winding up to their evening razzle, and the odd single man, but thus far no lone female lawyer hunting for a D-list TV celebrity to rook. The clock ticked on and he got thoroughly sick of the over-salted fries, yet had to order more because otherwise the staff started aggressively cleaning near his table to get him to move on.

I'll wait until ten, he decided. His patience lasted until precisely twenty-five minutes past nine, after which he decided he'd been stood up and, though he had known the whole thing was a scam, somehow that was still galling. The only extra icing this turd cake could garner, in fact, was if he got home to find his flat had been turned over

I am a joke, decided Felix 'Harry' Bodie. *This is what my life's come to? Cloak and dagger bumblefuckery as I try to outmanoeuvre a fake solicitor who's likely just stolen my telly.*

He left the restaurant and stepped out into the chill evening air. *Just another damn thing to put behind me. Fools and madmen.* And then a piping voice was calling, "Mummy!"

There was a child of maybe seven or eight and they were pointing at him and dragging at the hand of their harassed-looking parent. Their eyes were huge, as though it wasn't an actual human TV presenter they'd met, but one of the animated crime-fighting dogs or maths squirrels from the programs Harry introduced. Their evening, apparently, had just been made, and they were virtually exploding with excitement.

Harry and the mother exchanged a look that explicitly included the possibility of gaslighting the adorable tot by pretending that he wasn't, in fact, Harry Bodie, and possibly that there never had been a Harry Bodie or even a BBC. But the avalanche of the child's glee swept all such alluring possibilities away and instead Harry ended up kneeling down with his best cheesy presenter's grin and having his photo taken with the kid. And when he straightened up, he saw Seitchman.

He knew it was her. The face fit the voice, somehow. A short, compact woman in a tweed coat, looking right at him with an expression of tactical superiority. While he'd been staking out the door to the Bombay Sapphire, so had she. And she'd been more patient than him, and now he'd blown his cover like a bad spy.

In retrospect, Harry would find it hard to explain to anyone why he just took off at that moment. Just started walking briskly away. He hadn't been in danger. Nobody was about to pull a gun. It was, perhaps, that Seitchman had been sat somewhere patiently watching for him all that time. And, yes, he'd been doing that too, but she'd been better at it, and abruptly he decided the whole business was too problematic and no longer any fun and he wanted out.

As he turned the corner he glanced behind him, expecting her to be stood down the street watching. She wasn't. She was following him. At a walk ever so slightly brisker than his own. Her hands were in her coat pockets. The thought of the gun—previously only existing as a patent negative— jumped back into his head.

There were a small number of people who were absolutely incensed about the *Underhill* books, he knew. They were mostly religious nuts in the States, and it seemed unlikely that any of them had somehow come to the UK and then impersonated a lawyer to bring him to a very public place so they could shoot him. On the other hand, if someone did thread the needle of all those unlikely things, he might still end up shot. And there'd been a faun in the garden, and so who was to say what could or couldn't happen?

Once he was around the corner, he actually started to run. Took more turns. Put distance and confounding choices between him and his pursuer. He wasn't thinking straight, he knew. He just had the sense of the world tilting, of him starting to slide away off it, in a way that only running would prevent. And maybe Seitchman was like the faun. Maybe that phone call had never happened and the woman hadn't been standing there.

He ended up with a burning stitch and a dangerously hammering heart two streets away, where the shops turned from malls and chain clothing brands to newsagents and fried chicken joints. And that was where he ran into Seitchman. She was standing in the light of a greasy spoon diner, hands in her pockets still, not even out of breath. There was a slight smile on her face.

"I mean, the Sapphire was more salubrious," she said, "but here's fine, Mr Bodie." She was a few years older than him, he reckoned, grey-touched fair hair tied back, face lined. Utterly implacable.

"How did you get ahead of me?" he gasped at her. Right then, the option of further high-speed perambulations was just not on the table.

"I jog every morning." She shrugged. "Also, you basically did a circle. I saw you running back towards me. Come on, let's talk."

"What sort of a lawyer are you?" he demanded wheezily.

She looked around as though worried about being overheard by the Bar Council. "All right, look, I'm not actually a lawyer. That just seemed to be a better way to get your interest."

"You what?"

"In my experience, people want to talk to private investigators even less than lawyers."

Sheer incredulity ended up with the pair of them sitting almost knee to knee across a narrow strip of table in the greasy spoon, secrecy overcoming social distancing.

"You're an investigator?" Harry echoed. "You're investigating me? Who for?"

"Can't say." Seitchman seemed oddly hesitant about actually getting down to things, now she had him there. "Mr Bodie, it won't surprise you that my client's interest was kindled by the revelations coming out of your recent—"

"*How Even Me?* right," Harry agreed sullenly. "But you're not press. You don't want an interview. So what is it? I mean, I won't lie, I have all sorts of crap going on right now and I don't need the complications."

"Your grandmother had quite the legacy," Seitchman said. "The books mean a lot to a lot of people."

"Sure, sure, treasured childhood memories."

"Grown-up people. Not just the halcyon days of innocence, Mr Bodie."

"Is… what?" Not how he'd expected a PI to talk, honestly.

"My client takes Underhill very seriously indeed." And she said it oddly. There was a way you used the word, when you were talking about the series—and then there was the way she said it.

"*Underhill*," he qualified.

"Underhill," she contradicted him. "The place."

"The fictional place."

"Well, obviously," she agreed reasonably. And then undid that by adding, "Isn't it?"

"Underhill, the fictional place that turns up in the fiction books written by my—grandmother." He almost said 'my fictional grandmother' which would have rather sabotaged the point he was making. "Is most definitely fictional, yes."

"What if I told you," Seitchman said, stretching the showmanship to breaking point, "that my client believes otherwise."

"Then your client is nuts," Harry said flatly. Very little of this evening had been funny, but right now it was getting even less so. "Or else your client thinks *I* am even more nuts than I am. And as the mental health of my family was the tabloids' dirty laundry recently, this is all in very bad taste." And he stood up decisively.

"There's something my client wants you to see," Seitchman told him. "They'll pay. A little, at any rate, but then just going to see something isn't too taxing. Easier than being on the telly."

Three or four complex, sarcastic rejoinders arrived in Harry's head all at once, becoming a hopeless snarl of angry words snapping at each other. In the end he just said, "What?"

"Mr Bodie." Seitchman leant forwards over the table, almost knocking her coffee over. "I want you to come and see a wardrobe."

He stared at her, then let out a strained bray of laughter.

"Your client," he got out, "needs to do their research. We're not the wardrobe one. That's the famous one. We're the other one. You need to talk to the Lewis estate. I'm sure they'd be delighted to come look at your client's wardrobe. Probably they see hundreds of them every day. Just in case, you know. I mean"—getting steadily shriller and unable to stop himself—"you'd want to know, wouldn't you? Or else someone in Hackney might get eaten by a lion and then where would we be?" And with that somewhat garbled riposte he stormed out of the diner onto the street, where someone shoved a bag over his head and bundled him forcefully into a car.

In all the confusion nobody saw what happened to the Odlin King's wand. When James and Wish Dog came back from pursuing the last of the villains, they found Gombles holding it up to the moonlight. His big eyes were wider than ever as he admired the silver dragons that chased each other up and down the wand's length.

"Gombles!" cried James. "Whatever you do, do not wave the wand!"

"Wave the wand?" Gombles answered promptly. "I shall!"

Though they shouted at him to stop, he twirled the magical artefact merrily about in the air...

The Seven Tasks of Underhill (1950),
Mary Bodie, Golden Century Press

CHAPTER THREE

THE WORST THING about it was the bag. Admittedly it was jostling elbows with a lot of other worsts because he'd just been bagged and stuffed in a car, and someone sitting next to him clouted him hard across the side of the head when he tried shouting for help. He sat back, dazed, the punctuated glimmer of streetlamps filtering through the fabric of the bag. Which was a pillowcase. A child's pillowcase from some considerable yesteryear; quite the vintage item, in fact. He knew because he'd happily eBayed his own for beer money about ten years before. It was a piece of *Underhill* memorabilia produced after the cartoon run. It was the one with Gombles the Clown on it.

Granma Magda had very much considered Gombles the Clown to be children's comedy gold. A laughing, inept goofball always doing the wrong thing to hilarious effect. 'Gombles, don't do that patently stupid thing!' they'd cry, and 'Do it? I shall!' he'd chortlingly respond. It was the single running joke of the series and Harry wondered whether anyone, be they ever so young, had actually found it funny. He certainly hadn't. Even on the page, there had been something off about Gombles. Harry felt he could look into the bumbling character's eyes and see an echo of his own desperate life, trapped behind the TV screen with a permanent manic grin as he wasted ninety seconds of his audience's lives between cartoons. And when the actual *Underhill* cartoon had come out, they had produced something truly special. Those vast moonish eyes. That grin that went so far past the clown's ears that the whole top of his head should by rights just zip off.

Every flash of streetlamps imprinted the image of Animated Gombles onto his retinas, until he just screwed up his eyes against the nightmarish sight. Until the fact of being kidnapped paled into comparison and the only thing worse would be if they took the bag off and he found a real Gombles goggling and leering at him. And if that happened, Harry decided, he would just die on the spot and it would be a mercy.

Around that time, he remembered that cop show where someone got kidnapped like this but ingeniously listened for clues from outside the car, so they could work out the route they'd been taken. Also just then, the car stopped and he was manhandled out. So much for that. They whacked his head on the side of a doorframe bundling him in somewhere. He was half-expecting the cavernous echo of a warehouse or somewhere similarly remote where horrible things could be done to him without anyone being any the wiser. What he got was a small room where a carful of people tried to shove him onwards, tripping over shoes and getting snarled up in hanging coats. And then another room. And a sofa. Definitely a sofa. People had hold of his arms still, but not too tightly. He reckoned a sudden heroic effort could see the bag off his head and himself out of... wherever. Except *wherever* sounded crowded. A murmur of voices, a dozen at least, men and women. Some of them were expressing concerns about the whole man-with-a-bag-on-his-head. Some were excited about it. Some were asking if it was the right man.

A gavel rapped. An actual gavel, calling the meeting to order. *Silence in court!* Harry had been braced for a desperate lunge for freedom, but now he froze, bizarrely cued by the sound to await developments. And then the bag was drawn off his head and he flinched from the sight of...

A rather nice upper middle class living room. There were three entire sofas in there without making the place cramped, and the drawn curtains over the big bay windows were of the same dark green velvet as the seating arrangements. There were glass shelves of tasteful ornaments and occasional tables and bookshelves and footstools and basically a lot of *stuff*. All of it good stuff, expensive, collectable, but still too much of it. And what there were also too much of were people, all of them looking intensely at him.

They did not look like a dangerous gang of kidnappers. They looked like a dangerous gang of bank managers. Most of them were in the latter reaches of middle age or well into retirement, and the old boy with the gavel was surely closing on seventy. The remaining handful were decidedly younger and beefier, including the men on either side of Harry, presumably the active kidnappers. The more he looked at them, the less he could work out what this was about.

"Mr Bodie," said a plump woman wearing a dog collar. A matronly-looking vicar, in fact. Offering him a cup of tea. With a little sugar-speckled biscuit.

"I am…" Harry said, "not sure what's going on." He took the tea and biscuit, staring at both with deep suspicion.

"Mr Felix Bodie, a.k.a. 'Harry' Bodie," intoned the older man with the gavel, "it is my great pleasure to welcome you to the two hundred and ninth gathering of the Esteemed Company of the Underlings."

Harry stared at him blankly. "Underlings," he repeated. "Aren't they the… little yellow guys from that film, or…" Apparently not, from their looks. "Or is it like a dominant-submissive thing, or…? Wait…" Because an insistent memory was surfacing. Not something he'd ever run into, but his mother had been complaining about letters from some crackpot self-made fan club. A bunch of grown people, she'd lamented, taking gran's books far too seriously, asking all sorts of weird questions. Wanting to know things as though it was all *real…* And she'd had to get a lawyer, he recalled. Had to actually take one of them to court, because he'd turned up at the house and… Harry hadn't even been born, then. It was all fragmentary recollections rattling about in his head.

"You kidnapped me," he told them. "I mean… you actually *kidnapped* me. I was… I mean, if you wanted me to sign something for you, or do a talk, or…" Without the tea and biscuits he'd have been ranting, before leaping bodily through the window. But that would have involved spilling the tea or even breaking the delicate china cup. Somehow his residual politeness got in the way of doing what, in any other circumstance, would have been entirely appropriate.

"I'm afraid not, Mr Bodie," said Gavel. He had the sort of plummy voice you get from private education and a lifetime of getting exactly what you want. Harry reckoned he was a retired High Court judge from the way he played with the little hammer. "After all, you're only the *grandson*. *Your* signature wouldn't be of much value to us, now, would it?" In the same tones he'd probably used to deride a defendant's alibi. The man settled back in the plush armchair he was monopolising, balancing his own teacup and watching Harry with a keen eye. "I know what you're thinking, Mr Bodie."

Harry wasn't sure he himself knew that, and was keen to be enlightened.

"You're wondering why we waited so long."

It honestly wasn't what Harry had been thinking.

"We've been biding our time, no need to hurry matters. But then you had to go on national television explaining the true provenance of your great-grandmother. Did you really think that the word wouldn't spread to other ears, Mr Bodie? There are parties taking an *interest* in you. We had to accelerate our plans."

"Uh-huh." Harry bought time by eating the biscuit. His eyes ranged about the room. Everyone there was dressed better than him. There were pearls and bespoke suits and Italian leather shoes on display. "Plans," he noted, dropping crumbs onto the sofa and seeing a couple of them wince at the poor form. "Which are what, exactly?"

"Why, Mr Bodie, you're going to take us home with you. And in return we will restore you to your rightful place. As King of Underhill."

Harry realised he'd put his default smile on. The one he used for professional purposes when smiles were called for and he was feeling anything but smiley. It was the one he used for the purposes of telling seven-year-olds 'No, go on, please do tell us more about this impenetrable blot you've drawn which is supposedly me,' or listening to production company executives outline their 'vision.' Everyone was watching him very expectantly, though, and he wondered if he was supposed to leap up crying, 'For God, Elizabeth and the crown!' and lead them off into nowheresville right then. Instead he said, with creditable restraint, "You do realise that Underhill is a fictional place, don't you?" *I mean, I've literally had this conversation with an adult twice in the same evening, and that's two times too many in a lifetime.*

"Come now, Mr Bodie. The world at large is free to believe that, but we know better..." The judicial old man trailed off thoughtfully. "Can it be that you don't know?"

Infuriatingly, there was actually a certain amount of upper middle class smirking going on, as though it was *he* who was deluded and *they* who were the rational ones. The younger man to Harry's left jabbed him painfully under the floating rib.

"He's covering up. He *can't* not know."

"No, no." The old man leant forwards. "I do believe his confusion is genuine. Did your mother not tell you, Mr Bodie? Or is it possible that Magda did not tell *her*?"

"They're just books," Harry persevered gamely. "Children's books. For children. I told it to your private eye and I'm telling it to you."

"Private eye?" The younger man poked him again. "We don't need to hire private eyes."

"It's the *others*," the vicar said. "We acted just in time." She actually clutched her pearls.

"Mr Bodie, the books are just books, yes," the old man said to him. "But Underhill is real."

THEY TOOK HIM to a… possibly it was a shrine. A room at the heart of what was obviously an expansive suburban mansion, a couple of million quid's worth of real estate, and someone had done one room up as an Underhill museum. There were glass cabinets with first editions, even some yellowing annotated manuscripts. Framed book covers from a variety of editions and translations; a cabinet of the weird gachapon figures that had come out in Japan in the '90s for no reason Harry had ever been able to disentangle. A display of '80s merchandising: lunchboxes and stickers and child-sized pyjamas folded neatly. A great big image of Gombles the Clown from the cartoon, louring down with colossal round eyes, and he could have done without that. The whole thing gave him the creeps.

The old man was opening one of the cases and taking out a manuscript, bringing it over to a lectern. He seemed genuinely aghast at Harry's ignorance. "Mr Bodie, if you really don't know, then we need to educate you quickly. As I said, we're not the only people with an interest. Come here, will you?"

And Harry wasn't being forcibly held anymore, but the whole crowd of them were right there. And anyway… when someone says 'Come here, will you?' and wants to show you something, and it is manifestly about *you*, what option do you have?

They had the manuscript open, an early draft on Granma Magda's old typewriter with the defective B. It wasn't only annotated in her spiky handwriting, but had several other passes in various neater scripts. Pencil, copperplate, red biro. There were words underlined and little grids of letters where someone had been determinedly decoding text that Harry was certain there were no codes within. There were odd symbols that reminded him of astrology, little diagrams of circles and pentagrams and arrows.

"You see, don't you?" the old man said.

Harry's professional smile was still effortlessly in place, but his bafflement must have leaked out through his eyes, because everyone there was looking very disappointed.

"He's completely clueless," the rib-jabbing man said.

"Give him a chance. He'll get there," the vicar decided, and patted Harry's arm consolingly.

"You are all—" started Harry. *Mental. You're all mental.* Except that wasn't exactly language he should be throwing about, given his own family history. "Really confusing me," he settled on. And at least nobody was talking about hurting him. And there had been mention of restoring him to a *throne,* even. And the throne didn't exist, obviously, but that at least removed a sense of threat from this weird coterie.

They descended on him and, over the next hour, educated him furiously about the Real and Secret Nature of Underhill. The old man took a back seat while the vicar led the charge. They took him through the complex annotations, each layer of them. They told him earnestly about their own personal experiences when, in a golden childhood hour, they had glimpsed past the veil of apparent normality to peer into Underhill's hallowed groves. How this old woman had, as a girl, met what she insisted was Wish Dog, but which Harry reckoned had probably been just Dog. How the vicar had heard a mysterious voice intoning the Royal Creed of Underhill in her bedroom. How the younger man with the proddy fingers had found himself briefly in Underhill after a 'ritual magic exercise' into which phrase Harry inserted the word 'mushroom' between the second and final words.

It was all rather sad. They all seemed to have some story to tell, and those stories were all from years or decades before—half a century, in the case of the old woman. They'd all read the books at an age-appropriate time, and somehow those stories had never stopped being part of their lives, childish things they hadn't put aside when they grew up. And that young belief, the desire that Underhill be *real*, had sat in them and fermented with age, until... this. Until they were a group of comfortably middle class people, doing perfectly well for themselves, clearly more than functional in modern society. Except behind the posh houses and the smart clothes was a weird mental abscess. They *believed*. They all genuinely believed that Granma Magda's books opened onto something to which he could somehow lead them. Where he'd be king and they'd be... what? He had no idea what these 'Underlings' and the land of Underhill would actually do with one another in the impossible eventuality that they should meet.

The patent nonsense of them was warmly reassuring, positioning him far more towards the 'rational' end of the sanity spectrum. And yes, he remembered he'd run into a horned man outside the flat. And, right now, he could dismiss even that as a sign he should drink less. When it was just the cadaverous faun alone, it was a terrifying anomaly. Now the image had to share a podium with this pack of overmonied loons, the threat rubbed off. He could imagine the terrifying figure shuffling embarrassingly and trying to explain, *they're not with me, mate...*

Later on, when they'd all told him their treasured moments of epiphany, he ended up alone with the old gavel-rapper in a well-appointed study, shelves lined with leather-bound books, great big desk, the whole business. He was Geoffrey Warrington, apparently, and he was the Underlings' current Magister, which was their made-up name for the leader of the made-up thing they were.

"I can see what you think, Mr Bodie," Warrington said, smiling. Some rather good port had been broken into, which had further eaten into the panic of the original kidnapping. This would always be remembered as a very weird night, he reckoned, but at least it was turning out to be harmless.

I think you're all off your rockers, was what he actually thought, but he was all prepped to say something politic like, *I think you all really love my grandmother's books*, when Warrington went on, "You think we're mad."

"I..." Harry settled for shrugging.

"The others can be a little enthusiastic." The old man smiled. "You'll appreciate we can't be that choosy. There aren't that many people like us who believe. It's hard to source new recruits." And that *people like us* was plainly being used in the same way it might at an exclusive golf club, and Harry was not actually a *person like them*. But apparently his heritage made him an honorary *us* and the port really was very good.

"It was different when I joined," Warrington explained lugubriously. "The Magister back then had known Crowley. He'd come to the Underlings out of occult circles. These days it's all that dreadful television stuff, or just the books. They don't understand the nature of Underhill." He leant forwards suddenly, gripping Harry's hand with his dry fingers. "They're not interested in the underlying *truth*."

Harry, who'd thought Warrington was leading him *up* towards normalcy, now understood he was being led further down. "Truth, right," he echoed.

Warrington got down one of the larger, crumblier-looking tomes from the shelf, opening it at a ribbon to reveal a drawing of a bearded man in a big hat who looked like Shakespeare's angry landlord. Across the page from him was a rather rougher woodcut of a man surrounded by glassware and standing in a sigil-inscribed circle.

"This is Emperor Rudolf the Second of Bohemia," said Warrington, of Angry Landlord, "whose court drew to itself every learned scholar of magic and the occult sciences that Europe had to offer. And *this,* Mr Bodie, is Carolus Svoboda." He paused dramatically, and Harry had a moment's frowning before he remembered the name his great-grandmother had been booked into the asylum under.

"Carolus Svoboda," Warrington repeated. "An alchemist. A man who rubbed shoulders with Dee and Nostradamus. And, rather than seeking the elusive philosopher's stone, his surviving writings tell of his obsession with finding a gateway into faerie by scientific means. Look." Turning the page to show a photograph of an even older document: illegible writing, diagrams, pictures of naked women holding up flowers. "These are some of his calculations," Warrington explained-without-actually-enlightening. "He set it all out. How he would open a path to the otherworld. He came back to England with Dee. And then he disappeared, Mr Bodie. No more was ever heard from him. He's barely more than a footnote in history. Except, three and a half centuries later, a woman comes from nowhere—speaking a mingling of antique Latin and Bohemian!—and ends up in the London County Asylum. A woman who claims to be heir to a faerie kingdom, and whose name is given as Divaty *Svoboda*. Do you think that can possibly be a coincidence, Mr 'Bodie'?"

Yes, Harry thought. *I absolutely do*, but he didn't say anything of the sort because there was a deranged fire in the old man's eyes, and he didn't want to get burned.

"Your great-grandmother, Mr Bodie. Whose stories were later immortalised in the books her daughter wrote, and which we have all enjoyed, but they are, as you say, just fiction. Just a mangled account of the true wonders that Carolus discovered and claimed for his family. But the magical land is real, and your family ruled there for generations, and you can take us there." His smile was probably meant to be kindly and encouraging, but it chilled Harry to the marrow. "Now, are you ready to drop the pretence? I understand that you have kept your secrets for a long time, but you're among friends here. You are among your future subjects and followers, Your Majesty."

"Look, Mr Warrington. Sir. I..." For a moment he was going to play along, but the whole thing was too insane even for that. "I'm flattered, I really am." As though he'd been offered an after-dinner engagement for far too little money that he really didn't want to do. "I don't have any magic way into fairyland, though. If there was ever anything there—I'm not saying there's not, I'm saying *if*—then it's not come down to me. Mum never told me any secrets, and nor did Granma Magda. I'm sorry. It's fascinating, it really is, all this, but..."

"You really don't know, do you?" Warrington noted sadly, then he pitched his voice up suddenly. "Peter, would you come in here."

Mr Rib-jabber must have been right outside the door, because he sauntered straight in at the call.

"I've sent the others home," he said, and there was a soft eagerness in his voice that Harry really didn't like. "Told them we'll let them know next steps on WhatsApp later in the week. He's not cooperating, then?"

Warrington nodded dolorously. "Mr Bodie appears ignorant of the mysteries," he said. "Mr Bodie, in all fairness, you should know that I am the pre-eminent scholar of Carolus Svoboda's work, and Mr Thistlesham is, as well as a successful merchant banker, a ritual magician of no mean skill. Between us we have devised a means by which Underhill might be reached. With your assistance."

Harry decided that Peter Thistlesham did indeed look like a merchant banker. This assessment only intensified when the man leant in the doorway with ostentatious menace and said, "It's all in the bloodlines, you see," putting untoward stress on the word 'blood.'

"This ritual magic business..." Harry started.

"You must understand we would far rather achieve our ends with your cooperation," Warrington said. "Ideally, we would want you to take up the throne on the other side. Carolus indicates the land must have a king to avoid falling into ruin, you see. And you are the sole survivor of his line. But we can survive a little chaos. We will, after all, be entering Underhill with all possible modern advantages. I believe the inhabitants will have no choice but to submit to us."

"Uh-huh," Harry said weakly. "And this ritual magic

business," because his mind really had caught on the hook of that 'blood.'

"I am hopeful that only a token offering may be required," Warrington said. Thistlesham's expression suggested that he wasn't hopeful of any such thing. Thistlesham, in that moment, looked like the sort of man who'd bathe in the blood of virgins every Tuesday if only you could source it from Waitrose.

"Right, then," Harry decided, and made a determined break for it. He reckoned he could power Thistlesham out of the doorway and then just run around the house until he found a door or a window he could exit through. What actually happened was that his rather flabby, untoned form bounced off the rock-hard physique of a man who plainly dominated the squash courts and went to the gym every morning. When Harry ended up right back in the chair he'd got up from, Warrington had a gun. An actual gun, an automatic pistol very definitely pointed at him.

"I don't want to have to hurt you," the old man said, "but I *do* want to go to Underhill. And after your ridiculous stunt on the television, we're running short of time before someone else finds you and we lose our only chance. And so it comes down to this. I'll give you tonight to think back on everything your grandmother ever told you about Underhill, because there *will* be a way that you can access it. And failing that, we'll have to try Peter's way, and see just how much blood will be necessary."

The entrance to Smackersnack's lair was between two great old trees so shrouded in silk that the webs made a tunnel. The tunnel fell into darkness and roots stuck out at crooked angles like fingers. James brandished his sword in his right hand, and Jemima had the lantern in her left, and their other hands clasped tightly.

"Smackersnack!" called James. "Will you come out to parley?" but there was no answer from the dark.

"I do not want to go in there," Jemima whispered, thinking of the great bulk of the terrible spider lurking in the blackness, waiting for them.

"We must rescue Timon." James was afraid himself, but he made his face brave for her, and then took a step into the shadow of the tunnel.

The Lost Crown of Underhill (1951),
Mary Bodie, Reith and Baldwine House

CHAPTER FOUR

HARRY'S PLAN, INSOFAR as there was a plan, was that he should let Warrington and Thistlesham deposit him wherever they intended, and then simply break out the most convenient way and flee the property. Perhaps they'd stow him in a cupboard or a spare bedroom. He reckoned that ingenuity and a level head would serve to extricate himself from any of those places. He also reckoned that, although whatever Thistlesham the apparently-a-magician had planned for him might be fatal, they needed to keep him alive up until it happened. Hence wild shooting at his fleeing back would probably be counterproductive.

All of which went out of the window when they showed him the dungeon.

It was a nasty little room set under a flight of stairs, and half a level below the ground floor of the house. The door had a solid padlock. Inside there were no windows, nor furnishings of any kind. The floor was poured concrete and the walls were breezeblocks. There were stains on the floor and the room stank of stale urine and something that Harry felt might be despair. At the threshold, for all there were two men and one gun behind him, he balked.

"What is this?" he asked, dry-throated.

"Mr Bodie," said Warrington, still impeccably polite. "When one is serious about a certain kind of ritual magic, a degree of practice is required. Don't worry yourself about it."

The enormity of that last offhand comment had Harry spinning on his heel to shout into the old man's face, but Thistlesham shoved him in the chest as he did, and he fell into the room. When they slammed the door to, the little space was utterly lightless.

Naturally he tried ramming the door, but it was solid enough that his shoulder would patently give first. Other than that, he'd seen the room. There wasn't much of it and it was quite bare.

His life, he was forced to admit, had taken a decided nosedive recently. He would love to pin the blame on Margot Lorne and *How Even Me?* but he felt things had accelerated past that. There was this virus business casting a disproportionate pall over his whole profession. There had been the baffling meeting with Seitchman the PI, which now seemed like an amusing after-dinner anecdote, should there ever be another dinner for it to come after. And there was the faun, but right now, imprisoned in a little cell and waiting on the pleasure of a pair of self-professed magicians, that whole encounter seemed almost whimsical. Like a little fragment of memory left over from childhood. Not that he'd ever met any fauns in childhood. Not like James and goddamn Jemima, the unreasonably well-behaved protagonists of the *Underhill* books.

Warrington had mentioned Crowley, when talking about the founding of his little secret society. Harry had no idea how bad Crowley had actually been, in the sacrificing people stakes, but apparently this little clique had adopted the technique with gusto. He wondered whether the vicar was in on it, and how that worked precisely.

He hammered on the door and shouted that he remembered the way to Underhill after all. Not much to lose, let's face it. Tell them they had to take him somewhere. Manufacture a chance at escape. If he'd been thinking clearly he'd not have ended up locked up under the stairs in the first place. *Ah, yes, hindsight, always my weapon of choice.*

Either they couldn't hear him or they were already too invested in their nasty little business. Nobody came to hear his ingenious web of lies.

He stopped, and sat on the hard floor with his back to the door, breathing heavily. The dark was weighing on him, but mostly because his imagination was filling it with images of pentagrams and black robes and daggers. Although, given the provenance of these two, they'd probably do it in top hat and tails, with a Miyabi kitchen knife.

There was a bang. Not a gunshot bang, but something chunky and physical. The sort of sound that Harry might have looked for when he rammed the door, but which the solidity of its construction had absolutely scotched.

Someone's come! Someone's called the police! he decided. Maybe Seitchman had tailed his kidnappers to the house? He was instantly at the door again, banging and hollering for all he was worth, determined that any investigator wouldn't ignore the cupboard under the stairs in their search. Whatever happened next in the house at large—the demands, the challenges, the initial skirmish—was therefore totally lost on him.

When the screams came, he stopped. They were loud enough that they cut through his own racket. He heard a high voice, so twisted in pain it could have been Warrington's or Thistlesham's or anyone's. *Then* there were gunshots: one, then two more in rapid succession. He heard Warrington cry out, "Get back!" almost falsetto with terror. Then—Harry's ear pressed to the door now—a choking sound, and a brittle snap, deadened almost to nothing by the intervening wood. And a thud, that Harry's imagination was quick to ascribe to a body. And another, meatier *chunking* sound that had his imagination deciding it didn't want to play that game anymore.

And a knocking. One, two, cautious. Closer. A hollow sound like a staff on a bare floor.

And closer. Knock. Knock. Knock-knock.

Who's there?

On the other side of the door, something metal scraped. He leapt away, just managing to stuff the scream back down his throat. Suddenly he was very happy for any intruder to overlook the cupboard under the stairs.

The door rattled slightly in its frame, then the knocking

sounds resumed, receding. He breathed out a long sigh.

Of course I'm still stuck in the—

They returned, faster. He had been on his way back to the door, and now he just flattened himself against the wall, pushed right into the corner of the cell, crunched up as small as he would go.

There was a rattle. He understood. The wooden-legged intruder had gone to find the key.

He heard the dead thud as the now-released padlock hit the carpet.

The door creaked open, just a little. Painful light striped in, painting the stained floor and the barren wall beyond. Something stood there, just out of his sight. He willed it to remain so. He wasn't breathing. He tried to stop his own heart, in case the intruder could detect the beat.

He heard the long, ragged hiss of the other's exhalation. They sounded tired. Harry sympathised. They should probably go somewhere far, far away and have a lie down or something.

They left. He heard the knocking sounds, stomping off. And then a more distant clatter. And then nothing.

Waiting, and waiting, but still nothing. And the door was ajar, that blade of light bisecting the cell.

He took his shoes off. It was something he'd done in a police show he'd had a bit part in once. Stocking-footed, he padded out into the hall, and then into the...

Well, it had been a living room, last he'd been in there. The furniture had been shoved to the sides, though, and the carpet rolled back to make that bare floor he'd heard all the knocking on.

There was an actual pentagram of metal strips set into the floor, surrounded by inlaid sigils. He didn't give the workmanship the attention it deserved because of all the blood.

Geoffrey Warrington was lying close to where Harry had entered the room. His neck was at a very wrong angle, past ninety degrees from the sort of line one would generally prefer. His face was practically on backwards. All of which was nasty, but only won runner-up in the contest, because Peter Thistlesham had been gutted. He was lying in the centre of his own ritual circle. Someone had carved him up quite brutally. There were hacking wounds in his outflung hands where he'd tried ineffectually to stop them doing it, and then there were considerably bigger wounds in the rest of him after he'd failed to do so.

There was something thrust upright into his splayed corpse. The source of that nasty chunking noise, no doubt. Harry stared at it.

It was a sword. Not just any old sword, either. It had a ludicrously impractical two-pronged blade, like a can opener. Both curved tines were—well, still dripping with Peter Thistlesham, but also inset with lines of script that, Harry knew, would be gold if he wiped the gore off. He had no intention of getting close enough to read them, but they'd say, *In innocence and purity I'm drawn/ To fight the foes of righteousness forlorn./ Let none who justice love know woe or fear/ For Underhill, gallant Underhill is here!* The slightly dodgy scansion of the last line had always bothered him.

And probably Warrington, the Underhill nut, had

commissioned a replica from somewhere, and the intruder had just picked it up. But it stood there, driven through the corpse and into the heart of the pentagram, as though it had been left for Harry to find. *Whomsover draws this sword from this dead banker...* Except Harry was supposedly *already* the true heir, and so what...?

Something moved in the next room. Something large and formerly very quiet, whose feet—or something like feet—sounded like staves' ends being struck against the floor. Harry felt his heart contract with woe and fear so hard it physically hurt, and then he was rushing out of the living room. And then through the next room and the next, because he had no idea of the layout of the house, and Warrington's pile seemed endlessly sprawling, like a house in a dream where you run and run, and the *thing* only gains on you, and there's no way out. And the thing *was* gaining on him. And there *was* no way out. Every room he left, he heard the stilting footsteps of something entering. And he ran full tilt and it just strode and he couldn't leave it behind.

And then, just as in a dream, he was back in the living room/ritual circle/murder scene again, skidding in blood, and that dreadful tread behind him, and in desperation he took the big bay windows at a run, curtains and all.

The curtains were probably serendipity. They tore off their rail easily enough, and cushioned him from the subsequent storm of glass and splintered wood. He ended up in a back garden that extended out into moonless darkness further than he could see. But there were lights on in the house, illuminating a gate that must lead to the front.

He took it determinedly, stumbling and fumbling but slapping the latch open and fleeing alongside the house. There were windows, and light poured from them. In the corner of his eye he saw a determined shadow stalking inhumanly from room to room, pacing him exactly. Hunched, gangly, bloody to the elbows. His imagination supplied the details. He wasn't going to look.

He burst out onto the house's front garden and its winding gravel drive. Behind him, he heard the front door rattle as something pawed at the handle.

He ran. He ran a long way before he even worked out where he was. Then he called a taxi he could ill afford to take him to a hotel he could also not really afford, because things had got real and he had no doubt they knew where he lived.

HE INVENTED AN illness so he didn't have to be at work, and then work told him he didn't have to be there because of the real illness that everyone else was getting, after which the Prime Minister told him not to travel anywhere anyway, unless he had to, or had some other reason, such as a burning desire to see Barnard Castle. He invented a cockroach infestation as an excuse to shack up with Toby Rissler, an old acting buddy. Toby had a cramped flat, but his sofa was just about suitable for a week or two, and they spent a couple of boozy evenings complaining about the business and its vicissitudes, especially now. Harry brought up the spectre of Edgar in *Lear* and Toby, who'd been going through a dry spell, raised a beer bottle to the coming year and all the performing opportunities it would doubtless bring.

And Harry tried to come up with some options.

He couldn't expect that this would go away. His agent had already left three emails saying that weird types had been trying to get hold of him. He had a voicemail from his building manager telling him not to have his loud friends come bang on his door and shout at three in the morning. The world was suddenly interested in Harry Bodie, but it was the wrong world. A world of scary hallucinations, middle-class secret societies and murder.

And in the end, he had only one person he could turn to.

The number was still stored there, of course. Both from the original call and the three messages Seitchman had sent over the twelve hours after his kidnap. Just nondescript things: *Call me—Is everything OK?—Let me know.* As though she wasn't sure who might be picking up. When he called her, there was a definite pause between connection and the woman's cautious voice saying, "Hello?"

"Seitchman?"

"Mr Bodie?"

"It's me, yes. Look—"

"I saw you get snatched."

He tried to parse the words for any sense of her feigning innocence, but he honestly wasn't that much of a judge. "I notice you didn't call the police or anything," he said tiredly, leaning back into Toby's sagging sofa. "Or maybe you've been investigating privately?"

"I did call the police, actually," she said shortly. "They were very interested, and then they weren't interested. In a way that suggested someone high up had told them it wasn't interesting after all."

"Figures," Harry decided. "Look…" And he ran out of things to say. So that what came out next, rather than being cagey with her, was, "Are you an Underling?"

"Ah," said Seitchman, in a way that communicated very clearly she knew exactly what he meant. "Ah. No, I'm not. But I know of them. Just a snobby book club, basically."

"Really fucking no, they're not," Harry said, with feeling. "Look, this is your chance. Who is your client, and what do they want with me? I am looking at options, right now. I have been kidnapped and I'm basically on the run from I don't know what kind of crazy. What can your client do for me?"

Another pause. He tried to picture Seitchman, seeing her in his mind's eye in a trenchcoat, chain-smoking over a desk behind a door with her name on it. In New York in the 1930s. *Thanks, mind's eye.*

"I'm going to give you an address to meet me. Out of town. There's something there I can show you. It might answer some questions. It might, in fact, answer everything."

"That is a lot of 'might' for a plan."

"It's all I—and my client—have, Mr Bodie. If I was to say this wasn't an exact science it'd be the understatement of the century."

"What even is 'this'? The—the Underling lunatics, they wanted me to *lead* them to Underhill, to be the once and

future king or something. And then, someone came and…"
And led to a scatter of curiously muted news reports starting
Police are looking for… which somehow hadn't mentioned
much about the actual details of the deaths, or the dirty
great pentagram set into Warrington's floor.

A long sigh from Seitchman's end. "Look, Mr Bodie. I
could tell you. And you'd decide I was lying, or mad, and
not come." A beat. "And, you know, client confidentiality,
obviously," thrown in as a weird afterthought. "I can't
even promise that I can enlighten you in any way, with this
meeting. It's all I've got, though."

"You'll come alone?"

"I always work alone, Mr Bodie."

"You stand right in plain view outside the place. For as
long as it takes for me to be sure of you."

"If you must." And she gave him the address. It didn't
mean anything to him. A posh little village within striking
distance of Oxford, doubtless the retirement ground for
College dons and CEOs. Only when he was halfway there
on the train out of Paddington did he suddenly realise
where it must be.

He really was the sole heir to the Bodie name. His mother
had stopped at one, and Granma Magda before her hadn't
wanted more than a single daughter, and possibly that was
one reason why Grandpa Charles had separated from her.
Possibly, also, because she was more successful than him
and had set the book side of things up so that he couldn't
get at the money. Anyway, the two of them hadn't been on
speaking terms since long before Harry came along. Charles

Blaine had indeed remained in Oxfordshire, never remarried, and then died some time in the 'sixties. So, just perhaps, Seitchman's address was where the old man had ended up.

Harry did what recon he could. He arrived early, scoped out an impressively big sandstone-brick house in a beautiful little market town that positively reeked of money, paid far too much for an artisanal coffee, and waited. Seitchman turned up just as promised, just as alone, loitering outside the house, leaning against her battered Nissan, which must be the most downmarket car in the place. And Harry ran out of ways he could put off just walking out to meet her.

She looked up, birdlike, at his approach. "Ah, Mr Bodie," she said. "Good to see you well."

"You have no idea. After this, you're going to tell me everything you know about these Underlings."

She shrugged. "Sure. And then you can do the same for me, 'cause it sounds like you know more."

"This is Grandad's place, is it?"

"It was," she confirmed approvingly. "Right now it's owned by a nice family of four—the father's senior management at a pharmaceuticals company." She set off down the winding flagstoned path towards the front door.

"They're going to be delighted at us turning up, are they?"

"Well, it's my professional estimation that, so long as we're a bit careful, they never have to know," Seitchman said over her shoulder. At the front door, she took out a key and let herself in, bipping away at the alarm controls immediately inside. "I'm their cleaner."

"Huh?"

"Well, for today. Regular one called in sick. Terrible case of being paid under the minimum wage to clean a large house and then some random private eye turns up with a fistful of cash and says, how about a loan of that key and the codes to get in?"

She slipped in, and Harry ducked nervously after her. "Look—"

"You're going to suggest that some of what I do isn't strictly legal?" She turned to him with a cocked eyebrow.

"We're breaking and entering."

"Did you see me break anything? You ever hear anyone accused of just 'entering'? Trespass, a mere misdemeanour. Family's off on a lovely skiing holiday right now. We're fine."

For all her apparent sangfroid, she led him up the big staircase at a fair rate of knots. Not out of a worry at being discovered, but with a weird kind of excitement. Not unlike the Underlings, in fact. People closing in on a secret.

"Your client," he threw at her back as they ascended.

"Never you mind, Mr Bodie."

"They're another magician or something? They think it's all real."

"Isn't it, though?" She'd stopped at the top of the stairs.

Harry stared up at her. "I wish my grandmother had never written those damned books."

"And if she hadn't," Seitchman put to him, "would that affect the reality or otherwise of Underhill?"

Harry's mouth moved, stopped, moved, still empty of words. *She's one of them*, he thought. He was absolutely sure, right then, that there was no client. Or else that the client had infected Seitchman with that peculiar breed of madness the Underlings had been possessed by.

Upstairs, in a spare bedroom that had been turned into someone's poky little home office, was a wardrobe.

It was a big wardrobe. As wardrobes went, it was very impressive indeed. Lots of vegetal carving, twining knots of wooden foliage that almost seemed to form faces wherever you looked. Dark, old wood. Outsized for the room—possibly for the *house*. He couldn't imagine how they'd lumped it round the bend in the stairs.

"No," he told Seitchman. "I told you. That's the other one. With the lion. We didn't do wardrobes in my family."

"She had it made. Magda Bodie," Seitchman said. "I can show you the letters between her and the cabinet maker, in fact. She was very specific. Blaine, your grandfather, took it when they separated. Out of spite, I think. I can show you letters between them, too, where *this* is the thing she wants back. But she never got it. She wanted it for your mother, she says. Of course, you weren't on the scene then."

Actually approaching the wardrobe was proving remarkably difficult. There was a *presence* to the thing, a kind of reverse gravity, imposing an uphill gradient to the little room, forcing him away.

"Charles Blaine lectured at Magdalen, of course. He was a peripheral member of the Inklings. He knew Lewis well. And Lewis knew your grandmother. They may even have compared notes on the fictional worlds they were creating, though she wouldn't have been admitted to the Inklings herself, of course. No women, dontcherknow."

"Are you saying this is *the* wardrobe," Harry asked her hoarsely.

"No. That is a fictional wardrobe in a story. I am saying that this is the real wardrobe it might have been inspired by."

"But..." Harry heard his voice shake with the sheer stupidity of the question. "Why? I mean, why is there a wardrobe?"

"Because, Mr Bodie, if it was an occasional table, it would be very hard for you to get *into* it."

He stared levelly at her. "Into it."

"That is what one does, with a wardrobe." She was standing back from the offending furniture, hands in her coat pockets. He wondered if she had a gun, or if she was just trying to kid him that she had a gun, or if she just liked putting her hands in her pockets and looking casually menacing.

"It is not," he said reasonably. "What one does, is one stores clothes in them. Fur coats, if you must. One does not, as a rule, go into wardrobes."

"I would like you to try."

"Or what?" Waiting for the gun to make an appearance.

But the menace collapsed and she frowned and shrugged. "Or we've come all the way here for very little other than to look at a frankly overdesigned piece of early twentieth-century woodwork. I mean—my client has asked me if I would get you to go into the wardrobe. To see if anything happens. Look, Mr Bodie, I'll level with you. I'm working without maps here. My client is curious as to whether there is something *real* behind your grandmother's books. It sounds as though the Underlings were wondering the same thing. It sounds like maybe your grandma said some really interesting things to Clive Staples Lewis that got the mill of his literary creativity turning." She sighed, exasperated. "Or else it's all nonsense. Or else it's just a wardrobe. But unless you give it a go, how will we know?"

"Nothing's going to happen," Harry told her.

"That seems likely."

"Your 'client' is deranged."

A beat. "Yes, well. Probably."

"When nothing happens, I want you to tell your client just that. And tell the Underlings. And tell everyone else who comes calling. Sometimes a wardrobe is just a wardrobe. Sometimes books are just books. That's why we call it 'fiction.'"

"Except sometimes there's a place where fiction and reality meet," said Seitchman in an odd tone. "Folklore, myth, you know."

"That's just fiction that's old," he said shortly, and opened the wardrobe.

Any dramatic striding into it was complicated by the stacked boxes of old files someone had considerately filled it with, so he and Seitchman had an awkward ten minutes of lunking everything out and cluttering the floor with what looked like a hundred and fifty years of tax returns. After which the wardrobe was empty and he could quite clearly see the wooden back of it.

"You first," he suggested.

"What would be the point?" Seitchman asked. "If it works at all, it won't work for me. I'm not the promised heir to the magic kingdom. But I'll be right behind you."

"How comforting." Still slightly out of breath from the unloading, Harry squared his shoulders. "I am now going to step into the wardrobe," he told her. "I will, shortly after, step back out of the wardrobe, which is, after all, just a wardrobe. And then you can go tell the goddamn world that Underhill is just in books and I am not their free ticket to fantasyland."

"Sure," Seitchman said.

"'Sure,'" he echoed, and stepped awkwardly up into the wardrobe. Overbalanced. Tripped forwards, hands up to shield his face.

Fell forwards.

And further forwards.

Landing in the cold—a sudden chill far beyond an Oxfordshire winter. Thinking, *Fur coats, weren't there supposed to be fur coats?* And it was night, and when had *that* happened? The sky overhead was pitch dark, not a star in sight, yet no sense of clouds either. Just an utter dark unlike any sky ever, and he was racking his brains because, was it actually true that at no time in all the multitude of *Underhill* books did *anyone* ever mention moon or stars or celestial bodies of any kind? And yet he could see, as though a stagelight had picked him out. And all around, the white cold stuff that didn't quite seem to be snow. The stark black shadows of trees.

And *him*.

Standing in front of him, tall as life, wearing a ragged coat and threadbare scarf. Long, hollowed face capped with curling horns gleamed in the undirected light. Long tangled hair. Crooked animal legs, the hooves leaving little round prints in the non-snow as he approached Harry. Harry, on his hands and knees, frozen in shock, defenceless. Thinking of those hooves and of knocking sounds on wooden floors.

And then the faun—call him what he was, Timon the goddamned faun—folded down arthritically into a kneeling position; more complex than you realise, when your legs are built like a goat's.

"My prince," he said. "You have returned."

After the sounds of their pursuers had faded into the distance, James and Jemima circled back through the woods to where they had left the poor faun with the twisted ankle. The little creature crawled out of the tangle of briars he had been hiding in and thanked them profusely for their aid.

"What is this place?" asked Jemima.

"Why, this land is known as Underhill," the faun explained. He sat himself upon a rock and looked at his hoofed foot woefully.

"And who are you?" James said.

"My name is Timon, and I am very thankful that you came along, or else the Whifflers would surely have eaten me," said the faun.

"And what is that building there?" James pointed at the highest point of the land, past the tops of the tallest trees. The narrow spires seemed to reach almost to the pale gold of the sky itself.

"Why, that is the Great Castle of Underhill," Timon said. "And it waits empty for the rightful king and queen..."

The Road to Underhill (1947),
Mary Bodie, Golden Century Press

CHAPTER FIVE

"I'm..." HARRY TRIED to say, for form's sake, "not..." The words dried in his mouth. *I'm in Underhill.*

Rational Mind attempted to come to his rescue. *You're not in Oxford anymore. Doesn't mean you're in Underhill.* Except that was a bit like those theories about where life came from, that said it originated on another world and then came to Earth. Or that posited that God was the creation of some earlier ur-creator. Didn't actually answer the question 'Where does life come from?' or 'Who created the original creator?' Occam's razor suggested that one imaginary world was enough without bringing more into it. And there was the faun.

"Timon...?" Harry croaked.

The faun stood up. Possibly the expression on his meth-addict's face was a smile.

"Your Majesty, you honour me," he said. His voice

was cracked. So was the rest of him. He didn't look like the happy little creature from the cartoons, or any of the depictions on the various book covers, even that one time they'd got Edward Gorey in.

"I thought you'd be..." Harry said weakly, "shorter."

As he'd seen in the rose garden, Timon was taller than him. A cadaverous wasted hulk, all angles and concavity. He still wore the long flasher's mac, stained and torn and most definitely not Underhill in origin. The goatish hair on his crooked legs was moulting, bald in places. His exposed skin was an unhealthy grey-yellow, filthy and wrinkled and piebald with whitish, fungal patches. His expression...

Not, thank God, attempting the cheery grin of the cartoon, or else Harry might just have run screaming into the woods. A face that knew exactly the comparisons Harry was making, and was sorry for them.

"Come on," said Timon. "Let's get a fire going."

He strode away through the mounded heaps of snow and Harry floundered after him. Except it wasn't snow. It was cold, but not in the way snow was cold. It shifted, powdery, but not like snow did. And when more began filtering down from the utterly dead sky, it came like static, like dust. Cosmic dandruff. And the trees were... He hadn't even looked at the trees, what with the faun and the snow and the whole *Underhillness* of it all, but like Timon, the trees weren't well. Their dark bark was cracked and peeling away, and beneath it wasn't even wood but... something. A substrate that glowed a faintly lambent grey, striated with complex patterns, corroded and eaten into as if exposure to the air wasn't good for it. And, beneath that, a hollowness. As though the trees around him, that seemed simultaneously living and dying, were neither. Were papier-mâché over wire frames, except the outside wasn't papier and the frame wasn't mâché. But, most certainly, none of it was *tree* save that was the overall result.

He wondered if Timon was the same, inside. *He's a robot. Not a faun. Fauns don't exist. But robots do.*

The possibly-robot faun led him to a clearing in the woods where three great rocks stood, one of them overshadowing the other two at an angle. There was a fire laid there, and Timon squatted by it, his knees forced almost to the level of his ears by the effort. Harry was braced for a magic flash of fire or else a tedious round of whittling sticks together. Instead the faun produced an old plastic lighter and sparked away until he had the twigs going.

"You were waiting for me," Harry observed. "You knew where I'd appear."

Timon looked up at him. "It's always there. You know that."

"I…" But of course when you came in to Underhill, it was always to a particular glade. With a babbling brook and the green trees all around, and somewhere, up on the one high hill of Underhill, the castle in sight. Except it was too dark for the castle and nothing was green and the brook had probably frozen over or been buried beneath all the…

"What even is this stuff?" He took up a handful of the non-snow and it powdered unpleasantly between his fingers. Gritty, momentarily sticky, then evanescing away from his skin with a slick sense of chill. "What's with the cold? Underhill isn't like this. It's always green, in the stories."

"We were. It's been a while." Timon, robot or not, made every appearance of warming himself by the fire. It burned an unpleasant greenish-white, but then, what it was burning wasn't wood. Harry sat down beside it.

"What's going on?" he asked. "How did you get out, before? To find my keys, and... You know. Kill those people."

"You're welcome," Timon said, with a sidelong glance.

For the keys, or the murder? "This weird PI woman got me to go through a *wardrobe*, and now I'm—" He stopped. Seitchman had said she'd be right behind him. Either she'd been lying, or the wardrobe hadn't worked for her. He was on his own.

There was a long, mournful cry from out across the forest. Timon glanced up sharply, eyes narrow.

"There aren't any wolves in Underhill, either," Harry noted evenly. "Like with the snow and the wardrobe, that's the other place."

"Not a wolf," Timon said. "Wish Dog."

Harry stared at him. "I'm sorry, what? There's an actual Wish Dog? The best of all the dogs, lord of all canines, perfect exemplar of man's best friend?" He'd always found Wish Dog a bit saccharine, to be honest.

Timon gave him a look. Harry considered the difference between Timon-from-the-books and Timon-the-gangling-horror and then thought about Wish Dog.

"I don't want to meet Wish Dog," he decided.

"He wants to meet you," Timon said hollowly.

There was something else that the *other* book series had possessed that Underhill had previously been lacking, and that was a *treacherous* faun. Timon had been a lovable scamp always making trouble. This incarnation of him, though… "Let me guess," Harry said. "There's a reward."

Timon's gaunt face was all chiaroscuro in the firelight. "I'm still deciding."

"Whether to throw me to the hounds." Harry stood up, fists balled, wanting to run… somewhere. Except there was nowhere. There weren't even any tracks, because the non-snow didn't work like that. All around was just the dying or dead or non-alive forest and the sense that the entire world was slowly decaying towards a cosmic final entropy.

"We're not doing so well here," Timon told him.

"I can see that."

"We've been waiting for a long time."

"For *what?*" Harry demanded.

"For you." Timon unfolded himself to that improbable height again. "For the heir. A prince or princess of the blood, to come back to us. Ever since *she* left. Abandoned us just as her child was to be born. And we'd have taken care of her. We'd have had *adventures*. It was all ready. Everything perfectly prepared. And then *she* left, the child still in her belly, and there was nothing. Nothing but the waiting, and everything… getting worse." None of it accusing. Nothing angry about it. The full understanding that these events had taken place generations before Harry's birth. "And now here you are. And let us just say there is a difference of opinion as to what should be done with you."

"Wish Dog's hungry, is that it?"

And a new and unwelcome intrusion into their conversation, a saw-edged growl rolling out of the trees: "No. That is not it."

Wish Dog was the best of all dogs, of course. Large enough to ride on, with a glossy coat and bright eyes, a nose that could track forever, loyal and steadfast. Everyone loved Wish Dog. He was the truest friend a child could ever want, so redolent with virtues that a Wish Dog-fuelled *deus ex machina* provided the resolution for at least four of the *Underhill* books.

He'd seen better days.

There was a ragged crest of hair left down his spine, and other patches clinging on at random across his lean body. The exposed hide was blotchy, like Timon's, with fungal patches of slightly luminous blue-white, as though a radioactive mould was devouring him a piece at a time. Most of his happy, doggy face was gone. Certainly a great many teeth were on display even when he closed his mouth, a skull-rictus grin devoid of humour. His eyes rolled in flayed sockets, giving him a look of mute agony all the time.

This isn't Underhill, Harry decided. *It's* Five Nights At Aslan's. *Jesus.*

A little silvery medal, for valour in defence of the realm, dangled from his rotting collar.

"I'll take him now," Wish Dog said. The cartoon Wish Dog had spoken with proper lip sync, despite being a dog.

This monster didn't even *have* lips and the words came from somewhere deep in his throat, more growl than speech.

"I haven't decided if I'm giving him to you," Timon replied coolly.

"I'm right here," Harry pointed out.

Wish Dog padded further into the firelight, to nobody's particular benefit. "Little faun," he rumbled, "don't try me. What else were you going to do with him?"

"Hulder wants to see him."

Wish Dog flinched. "Don't get her involved, Timon. Just hand over the heir."

"I'm *right here*," Harry repeated. "I don't want to be *handed* to anyone. Talk to me, someone. Explain it to me. Let me help you, even."

"There's only one way," Wish Dog said, "that you can *help*."

"That's not what Hulder thinks—" Timon started.

"*Don't*," the dog snarled, "bring her into this. Just do your duty."

"Like a good dog?"

"Like me, yes." That cadaverous, permanent grin. "The best of all dogs."

"Oh, Christ," Harry whimpered. "God, Jesus Christ almighty protect me." As though he was still eight and going to a Sunday School that had adamantly *not* approved of his grandmother's books and their 'pagan nonsense.' *Why don't you read the nice one about the lion?*

"I'm sure you'll get him eventually," Timon said tiredly. "No matter what I do."

"Quite," agreed the dog.

"Just not yet." And the faun stooped and snatched up a stick from the fire. For a moment Harry thought he was going to hold Wish Dog off with a burning brand, but then he just lobbed the stick out into the darkness of the forest.

"Fetch!" he shouted, and Wish Dog roared, "You bastard, Timon!" and dashed helplessly after the missile. The best, after all, of all dogs.

"And now we run," Timon decided, and took his own advice so precipitously that Harry was almost left behind, floundering through the non-snow. The faun had to come back and drag at his arm, haul him in great leaping bounds through the drifts, between the trees.

"Where are we going?" Harry demanded, feeling his shoulder joint pull and grind.

"Hulder!"

"Who's—wait, the Tree Maid?"

"Don't call her that. She doesn't like it anymore."

Harry finally got his feet under him and managed to match the faun's helter-skelter pace. "And she wants to meet me?"

"She'll be coming to you even now," Timon confirmed, pausing to take stock and then dashing in a different but identical direction through the woods. "You're a beacon, my prince. There's no inhabitant of Underhill doesn't know you're here."

If Harry had needed anything else to give him a burst of speed, that did the trick, and for several desperate minutes he was even keeping up with the faun's long-legged lope as they ploughed through the powdery, curiously dry drifts, weaving through the dense maze of the piebald, decaying trees. In places, the whole forest had collapsed. Not just fallen trees: the earth had puckered in like a shrivelled sphincter and the trunks bowed towards it, their whole substance sloughing towards the epicentre. Where their bark and what lay below it had fallen away entirely, Harry glimpsed a kind of geometrical scaffolding like barbed chicken wire. Timon gave all such places a wide berth, and Harry was grateful for it. And yet the chase went on, stopping when he couldn't go any further, picking up the moment Timon judged he was rested. Hours of the monochrome hell of the forest, and the faun could have been leading him in circles and he'd never have known. And out in the darkness, every dilapidated denizen of Underhill, slowly homing in on the moving point that was him.

They plunged downslope into a dell where Harry was waist deep in the non-snow, wading grimly and waiting for the sudden drop into a depth that would drown him. They struggled up onto a hill where the trees leant away, and where a flat stone sat, white flecks flurrying across its smooth surface. James and Jemima'd had a picnic there, in one book or other. You could look across the valley and see the golden spires of the castle. He looked. There was only darkness.

"How long till dawn?" He sat on the stone suddenly, fatigue catching him by the heels and reminding him of all those times he'd said he would start going to the gym. "It's been ages."

"There's no dawn," Timon told him.

"What?"

"No dawn."

"What?"

The faun scratched at the base of his horns, frowning. "I can't really say it any more simply than that. What part of 'there's no dawn' doesn't make sense?"

Harry decided to ignore that. "You mean it's always..." *Always winter, never Christmas.* "Night?"

The faun shrugged, deadpan. "Is it night, though, if there's no day? I mean, there's a thing you have where you come from. Daylight saving time. That's what this is."

Harry was perilously on the brink of actually understanding something, and felt that would be profoundly worse than ignorance. He looked down over the forest—or at least the maze of trunks whose tops were lost in the overarching blackness above. At the great drifts of non-snow that extended as far as he could see. Which was far too far, given there was no conventional source of light. Either there was an invisible spectrum of light that the non-snow reflected back on a visible wavelength, or else it was luminous in and of itself. Like certain fungi and bacteria that were agents of decay, he thought, and shivered.

Some distance away, not far enough to be actually *in* the distance, there was a mournful howl. Wish Dog.

"He'll find us, of course," Timon said mournfully. "Like I say, everything will find you eventually. But hopefully he'll have to hunt around first."

"I thought he'd be right on our trail. That was always his thing, wasn't it? Best dog in the world?"

"Ah, well. He's not what he was. You saw how he's… deteriorated." And the faun put on an exaggeratedly posh old-time music hall voice. "'I say, I say, I say: my dog's got no nose…'"

"That," said a new voice, "is in poor taste, Timon."

The faun flinched, and Harry turned and beheld Hulder, the Tree Maid.

He'd had a complicated relationship with her as a character, when he was younger. In the books, she was the wise one who tended to turn up and patch wounds and give advice. She was a dryad, just as Timon was a faun, because Granma Magda, no less than CS Lewis, was heavily influenced by classical Greek myth. And then there had been the cartoon, and to the pubescent Felix Bodie there had most definitely been something about the curvy way the Tree Maid had been drawn that had stirred adolescent feelings in him. In much the same way others of his acquaintance had felt about that fox Robin Hood or one or other of the Thundercats. And now he turned, steeling himself, frankly, for horror and the death of childhood fancy.

And Hulder was beautiful. And terrible, but beautiful was still in there somewhere. Her oval face was still mostly smooth, save for the lightning flash of decay that reached down across one eye in a weirdly Bowie-esque touch. The twining tendrils that were her hair swept back in a mane from her temples. Her body lay in some weird valley between the asexual and the sexualised, like a manikin. It was woman-shaped, made of something that had originally looked like wood, and was now patched and marred by decay in a way that showed it had never been wood after all, nor any material Harry could name. She moved with a careful grace that only drew attention to Timon's angular awkwardness. Ghastly in her decay, and yet still attractive somehow.

"What have you done?" she asked, eyes fixed on him. Pleased to see him? Horrified? Impossible to tell from the composure of her features.

"Saved the world." Timon had sat down at the other end of the stone and was hugging his knees. "I don't know. There wasn't anything else to do."

"Maybe you should have done nothing."

"I did nothing for a long time. It didn't help." Timon wouldn't look at her. There was an old argument here, in which Harry was only an object, not a participant. "And there were others. They were going to kill him. And I gave him the sword." He looked at Harry mournfully. "Which I note you didn't bring with you."

"The... sword," Harry said slowly.

"The Royal Sword of Underhill. I left it for you. After I rescued you."

"The one covered in blood and stuck in a corpse."

"I didn't want you to miss it," said rascally Timon the faun.

"I mean, amazingly I didn't take it, no. On account of, you know, blood, fingerprints, police." A pause. "That was the actual Royal Sword of Underhill, was it?"

"The one and only," Timon confirmed sadly.

"Well, it's in an evidence locker now. In my defence, I didn't believe in Underhill. And... you'll forgive me for saying, this... this isn't..."

"Isn't the Underhill you were expecting," Hulder finished sadly.

"We've been better," Timon agreed. "By your own children's time, probably it will all have gone."

"Perhaps for the best," Hulder suggested.

"I'm not planning on having kids any time soon." A decision that entering Underhill had only reinforced.

"Well," Timon said tiredly, "that works too. I just wanted... *Do not go gentle into that good night*, you know?"

"You were doing your duty," growled Wish Dog, padding out of the woods. He stopped a respectful distance away from Hulder. "You all have a duty. To Underhill. To the blood."

Harry joined the dots in his head and was about to stand up and decry that these miscellaneous woodland monsters were basically just Warrington's Underlings working from the other side of the border, and that it was all about cutting his throat for a good harvest. Then Hulder had stalked forwards to confront the dog and he sat back down with a little bray of horror, because she was entirely empty. The back had come off her. From the crown of her head down to where the curve of her buttocks began there was just hollowness, a honeycomb of internal structure, a bioluminescent gleam of decay, and past it the concavities and contours of the inside of her head and torso. Her eyes stared backwards at him from the wrong side of her face.

"Christ," he whimpered.

"I will take him to the castle," Wish Dog announced. "Don't try to stop me. I will fix things. Everything will be good as new." And yet when Hulder took another step forwards, he backed off a little, though he loomed over her. Though his permanently bared teeth could have made kindling of her. The dog snarled and his exposed eyes rolled. "Timon. You brought him. Give him to me. *Please*, Timon. It can be good again." And despite the horror of him, there was a mournful need in Wish Dog that plucked at Harry.

"The king is the land, the land is the king, is that it?" he asked. "I mean, I'm here now and I don't see things getting better."

"That is why I have to bring you to the castle," Wish Dog agreed.

"Underhill must go on, Wish Dog?" Hulder asked softly. "Yes!"

"And us? Will we go on, once the heir ascends to the throne?" And perhaps there was some grand revelation on the heels of that, to make everything clear, but it was drowned by the terrible, apocalyptic sound that resounded across the forest. It was basso profundo, and vast as a foghorn, or a great tanker warning of its inexorable progress, save that it was a voice as well. A grand idiot hooting that shuddered the bark off the trees and set the heaps of non-snow shivering. All three of Harry's impossible companions tensed.

"He knows," Hulder said.

"I keep saying. Him being here's like screaming in everyone's head," Timon insisted.

Something was moving through the forest. Harry could

see it as a shadow across the scattered silvery gleam. He could hear it by the snap and crunch of the trunks as the mammoth creature shouldered them aside. That forlorn, monstrous voice spoke again, bellowing its wordless complaints to the bleak nothing of the sky.

"Who is it?" he asked, dry-mouthed.

And the answer he really hadn't wanted to hear, from Hulder: "It's Gombles."

Gombles the hilarious antic clown. Gombles the comic relief that only Granma Magda had ever found amusing. Bouncy little Gombles, with his big feet attached leglessly to the round bulk of his body and his string-thin arms weaving jointlessly, because the cartoon's artist had either no sense or far too keen a sense of visual horror. Gombles, who'd come up to about James' and Jemima's waist.

"What the fuck?" Harry got out.

"After the original went faulty," Timon told him, with a brittle cheer, "they made a new one. Only there was a scaling error."

Gombles howled again and the rolling lurch of his great sagging sack of a body smashed down another tree. The wan light of the non-snow extended up his form as he neared the hill, until it touched the raw white wounds that were his colossal, froglike eyes. They were fixed on Harry.

Hulder was striding forwards, holding up hollow arms, and Wish Dog just turned around and charged at the gigantic clown. The next flap-footed step the monster took just punted the luckless dog off into the darkness with a yelp. Gombles wasn't stopping for anything.

Harry ran. Just *away*, because he had no other reference. He ran downhill, at first because it was all downhill, and then because downhill should have been easier, except of course that was where the drifting non-snow had collected deepest. But he ran, and kept running, and the dreadful voice of Gombles resounded behind him. Perhaps he heard the shouts of Timon and Hulder, too, but right then he reckoned that was a *them* problem and not a *him* problem. He had his own problems, not least of which was discovering that not only was Underhill real, it was a bloody nightmare of epic proportions.

The forest was growing thicker ahead of him, but mere trees weren't going to impede the clown's Kaiju-style advance. A deeper patch of dark beckoned, though, and he thought it was a cave, or some structure where the trees bent together into a roof, a tunnel, somewhere the beast couldn't follow.

The thought of a boneless, clown-gloved arm snaking in after him was more than he could bear. He shoved on, fighting past heaps of blown non-snow, pushing at barriers of roots that stretched and gave, seeing the walls ahead dimly lit by trailing shrouds of faint luminescence, nets and curtains and…

He understood what he was looking at right at the moment the ground took a sudden downward turn and he toppled forwards ten feet and face-planted in a carpet of white, tangled threads. Plenty of the faintly glowing non-snow had found its way down here, but that wasn't what he was looking at. The cave around him was draped and hung about with ragged curtains and loops of webbing.

There had been a villain character James and Jemima had repeatedly defeated. A kind of mid-ranking monster, not a part of the major threats to Underhill's sovereignty but constantly turning up to make a nuisance of herself, and a meal out of various of the stories' minor characters. *They killed her, though*, Harry thought. *In* The White Sword of Underhill. Smackersnack, she'd been called. This was her lair, or one of them. He looked left and right about the web-messy cavern, seeing only the tangles and ropes of the great spider's work, encrusted with blown non-snow. His heart began to slow.

Safe from the goddamn clown, at least. And what then? What, precisely, was his game plan?

There were several tunnels out from this particular cave, but as they all went deeper into the earth and Underhill had lots of nasties sitting around waiting to be defeated by courageous youngsters, he didn't much fancy that. He wasn't that courageous, after all, and most definitely not young. And he had apparently turned down the chance to bring the fabled magic sword that made its wielder unbeatable and invulnerable, which was feeling more and more like a rookie error right now.

A sound came to him. A whispery little chuckle.

"Well now, well now, well now," it said. "What's walked its way into our webs, we wonder?"

Harry looked up, hoping for another scaling error, only in the other direction. A hand-sized talking spider was probably something he could defeat with his shoe, magic swords be damned.

She was easily as big as he was, just in the body. To get through to the outside must be a squeeze for her. His eyes took in the bloated abdomen, the armoured spikiness of her legs. The circular eyes like tarnished mirrors.

"Hello, handsome Harry," said Smackersnack politely. "Fancy finding a fine fellow like you parading into our parlour."

He was paralysed with fear right up until the point she moved. The moment she began to step daintily down from the ceiling, he fled. He ran back the way he'd come in, but she dropped down in front of him suddenly. He darted for one of the other tunnels, leading into utter darkness. Again, she headed him off, moving with terrifying nimbleness, and he jinked, took the last available exit, and tumbled into the black.

He had his hands out in front of him, fighting past ropes of web and clawing at coarse rock that crumbled like soft cheese under his touch. He had a horror of the whole substance of the place decaying in real time, and that one too many steps would see him just plunge into a quagmire of failed world. Behind him he could hear Smackersnack muttering contentedly to herself as she followed.

Herding me somewhere, he thought. And then, *Eggs, young. God help me.*

Then there was a thicker tangle of webbing barring his way, a dense knot of it almost like the drawstring of a closed sack. Whimpering with fear, he wrestled with it, as the spider patiently chuckled up behind him. He had no wish to hear what she had to say.

One of her legs plucked the webbing right above his head. He felt the sifting dust of it, picturing fangs the length of his forearm raised languorously to strike. With a convulsive jerk, he tore the tangle apart and tumbled forwards into…

For a long moment he was stuck—not simply caught in the web, but held paralysed, muscles rebellious, ploughing forwards into a jelly of air that seemed to have him suspended, and separated out his thoughts into disconnected chunks that his mind could barely cross between. A handful of experiential seconds that might have represented any amount of actual time. And then—

A confusion of boxes. Sudden, constricting space. Tight walls, agony in his back and legs and elbows from sharp edges and confinement. A vertical line of bright light. A man's voice, exclaiming.

Harry roared, actually *roared,* pushing back at everything that was pushing in at him. In his head, the spider was still right behind him.

He exploded outwards in a thunder of displaced files and boxes and broken wood. Splinters jabbed his hands and knees as he fell onto a carpeted floor. Carpeted with carpet, not with spiderwebs, and the bright, eye-searing light was a bulb, not the ghostly silver of the non-snow. And the voice demanding to know *What in the bloody hell?* was a man sitting at a computer, wearing a suit and tie. He stared at Harry, not unreasonably. So did the half dozen people in little boxes on his computer monitor.

Harry was back in the house, in the little home office. All around him was the wreckage of the wardrobe.

By the time James and Jemina found their way home to their grandmother's cottage on the edge of the wood, they were very worried. Surely, said Jemima, everyone would be very concerned about where they had been. James thought that perhaps Grandmother would have gone to all the neighbours and they might be out searching every field and copse of trees from her house to Mr Michael's farm.

When they reached their grandmother's doorstep, though, they could still smell the bread that she had been baking that morning, and so little time had passed that they had not even missed their lunch! Later, when they tried to tell Grandmother their adventures, she simply told them how wonderful it must be to have such an imagination. There had been a twinkle in her eye as she said the words, though, and James and Jemima whispered together that night about what Grandmother might have seen, when she herself was very young...

The Road to Underhill (1947),
Mary Bodie, Golden Century Press

CHAPTER SIX

"Hɪ," Hᴀʀʀʏ ᴛʀɪᴇᴅ. "How was the skiing?"

This failed to break the ice. In fact, it added a whole mostly unfathomable layer of frost to an already cold reception. The besuited man hurried his surprise visitor out of the incredulous gaze of the people on his monitor, and then downstairs, where they ran into the rest of the family. The whole neat little family, not on holiday, sitting around a table, everyone with a tablet or laptop. They stared at him, and a profoundly awkward situation was made both worse and better by the children instantly recognising him. His transformation from dangerous intruder to inexplicably present minor celebrity functioned as a kind of no-score draw.

Harry was trying to assemble some bizarre narrative, regarding a CBeebies special, surprise filming and his obviously being in the wrong house, and so sorry, please send a bill for the wardrobe to Auntie Beeb. The man in the suit seemed more interested in getting Harry out of the house as quickly as possible. While Harry felt this was within the range of reasonable responses, he was also surprised, almost disappointed, not to have the police called on him. He felt he'd earned an arrest. Some quiet time in a well-secured room might do him a power of good.

His phone, perhaps as a result of having gone considerably beyond the reach of his network provider, was dead as a brick. A request to use his impromptu host's phone met with a pop-eyed stare.

Just as he was stumbling away down the path, the man called him back to throw something at him, shouting, "And you'll want this!"

It was a surgical mask, Harry saw. He stared blankly at it. Yes, he'd seen people wearing them, off and on, with the whole virus-turned-epidemic that had been brewing throughout February. It seemed unusually generous of the man to present him with one, especially given the circumstances of their meeting.

Home, he decided. It was a long trek. Seitchman's crappy little car was, unsurprisingly, nowhere in evidence.

He took far too long to walk to the bus stop, and then the scrolling display showed far too few buses to Oxford, and in all that time he saw virtually nobody. The little village was weirdly vacant, as though the Rapture had been and gone, leaving behind only closed shops and a much-reduced public transport system. Nervously, he attributed this to the rural locale and it being office hours.

He was the only person on the bus. Or at least, he was after he'd agreed to put the mask on, without which the driver refused to let him board. He saw perhaps seven cars on the road all the way to Oxford, and the streets of the city were, if not deserted, then curiously depopulated. He asked the driver what was going on and the man favoured him with the sort of look reserved for idiots.

The train station was similarly deserted. There seemed to be half as many trains as usual. Everywhere there were signs and announcements about keeping distance and washing hands. Harry began to wonder if he'd come out of the wardrobe into the *right* real world.

The papers said there was a lockdown. They also said it was late March rather than the mid-February Harry last remembered it being. In which time the entire country had been transformed.

Always social winter and never Christmas...

The lost time should have been a shock. He had no idea where he stood with his employer, or if he still had one. He didn't know whether his bank account had contained enough money to meet its various outgoings for the past month or so, or all the other mundane demands of just being alive in the twenty-first century. He was put horribly in mind of those dreams about the cartoon characters failing at modern life. Because modern life was now, quite suddenly, alienatingly different to the way he remembered it.

The handful of other train passengers put as much space between each other as possible. One woman was furtively whispering on her phone as though to even talk at a normal volume might be contagious. Everyone else sat silent, mourners at a colossal funeral.

The paper was weirdly uninformative, quoting government spokesmen who were simultaneously saying that the plucky British public would pull through—that nobody should be worried and that everything would be back to normal and was under control—and also that the whole country was basically shut down, except for a baffling list of exceptions. And that nobody should go out or do anything, except for a different list of partially overlapping exceptions... Trying to parse the actual situation just from a day's slice of newsprint was like listening to the conspiracy talk of the Underlings; a jagged jigsaw of conjecture and make-believe stitched together and presented as whole cloth. And by then, Harry had been travelling and waiting by turns for too many hours, and before that had been running through a winter horrorscape pursued by dogs and clowns and spiders. *Some people, when they meet a treacherous faun in the woods, at least get offered tea and cakes.*

Although he didn't want to think about what kind of mouldering pastries Underhill might harbour.

Toby can fill me in, Harry decided.

Toby wouldn't even *let* him in. His friend's voice over the intercom sounded ragged and strung out. "It's all gone to shit," it crackled. "I don't feel good, man. I can't have anyone in. You'll have to go to your place."

"I can't go to my place," Harry argued with the door.

"Because—" And his mind was suddenly blank because he'd given Toby some sort of excuse as to why, but right then he couldn't even recall it. Not 'being in the middle of a gang war between merchant bankers and murderous fauns' certainly. "Look, Tobe, seriously, I have had a *time* of it, in ways you literally wouldn't believe. Help me out, will you?"

"You can't get *it* from cockroaches," Toby's voice helpfully filled in. "Look, man, I'm sorry. Nobody comes in."

He located a nearby motel. It was shut until further notice. He then spent far too long just wandering like a destitute around the streets, because the only option left to him seemed to be to actually go home, and he didn't know what might be waiting for him.

Eventually a police car drew up alongside and demanded to know what he was playing at. Harry had a muffled, masked conversation with the constable regarding his right to exercise, which he'd read about in the paper. The policeman then exacted his address from him and told him to go home. Which was just about the conclusion Harry had come to. Could the police give him a lift there? No, they bloody well couldn't, mate, don't take the piss.

And he stared at the constable's wild eyes, seeing a man who had literally no idea what the situation was or how he was supposed to enforce it, tilting between bullying Harry because he was there, and just driving off and pretending he wasn't. And somehow Harry didn't say, *I have some vital clues regarding two murders you might have heard of,* and he didn't say, *I was abducted by stockbrokers,* nor even

I've just got back from an imaginary world out of a kids' book and boy are my arms tired, even though his arms, and the rest of him, *were* tired. So tired he could just go to sleep on a bench, if only there had been a bench within a hundred miles that wasn't considerately designed to stop anyone doing just that.

Night preceded him to the flats, so that he made the final approach from the weirdly echoing tube station by the baleful yellow flare of the streetlamps. At least there was a moon. At least he could just about pick out a star or two past the actinic glare of the city. At least it was a proper sky and not the all-devouring void that Underhill got these days.

It had always been a bright summer's day, he realised, in the books. No night, no dawns or twilights. Always the best of all summer's days for James and Jemima to have adventures in. Always back in time for tea.

He paused at the rose garden, waiting to see who was going to leap out at him: mythological creatures, suburban cultists, private eyes. None of them did. Right then, with barely a whisper of traffic in earshot and not a soul on the streets, he felt as though he was the last man on Earth.

NOBODY MURDERED HIM in his sleep. Even the monsters who had dogged his steps over the last month were socially distancing. He charged his phone. All the texts and missed calls and emails of the last month failed to materialise. Somehow they'd fallen into the chasm between one world and the next and were presumably still receding like the Voyager probe, on an eternal mission into nowhere.

He called the production company. Apparently he still had a job, or would do when they'd worked out how he could safely do it. Some of his peers were talking about producing bouncy little home-filmed segments using their webcams. Living rooms across the nation were being done up as colourful home studios even as they spoke. Did Harry have a webcam? Maybe he should get one. It was the future of entertainment. Had he heard of Zoom? Nobody seemed to know what was going on, everyone told him contradictory things. He called his agent. His agent told him the world of the performing arts had nosedived to shit so quickly he wasn't sure if it would ever resurface. He was fielding desperate calls from his entire client list, actors and musicians were virtually breaking down his door demanding work and Harry reckoned he'd have been packing a suitcase for a midnight flit to somewhere if only that option hadn't also been taken off the table. In this universal miasma of panic and paralysis, Harry's having been literally out of this world for a month sank without making a ripple. He sat there as the straight man in a sequence of phone monologues and intrinsically understood that it wasn't his place to suddenly pipe up with 'I went to a magical land of horrible clowns and spiders.' Not because it would make everything worse but because, somehow, it actually *wouldn't*. He'd be criticised for introducing untoward levity into a serious global situation. 'Horrible clowns and spiders? Tch! We should be so lucky.'

The word that filtered down from on high was 'remain at home and await further developments.'

Harry awaited further developments. For a week after his return, he slept with a knife under his pillow, awaiting the Revenge of the Underlings. It seemed a fair assumption that there were others beyond their two casualties who had ritual daggers and spangly robes hidden somewhere, and either they'd want him for his precious bloodline or they'd want revenge.

Or else there'd be some other intrusion from Underhill itself, in the shape of a rotting hound the size of a horse or a bloody-handed remnant of Greek myth (or was all that Greek stuff just Underhill stuff that leaked out into the world thousands of years before?). They'd want him for... well, he didn't even know, but his mind was full of stories of that sort of mythic king who gets to lord it for a year and then gets sacrificed for a good harvest. He had no idea if that had ever actually been a *thing*, but it seemed to fit whatever role they had planned for him in Underhill.

Except nobody came for him. The knife-edge— literally—of tension lasted almost exactly a week before he accidentally slit open his pillow, and then got furiously drunk on whatever he had in the flat. He ended up shouting out of the window at three in the morning, challenging Underlings and fauns and Wish Dog to come for him, because otherwise it was the waiting, and he'd hit a hard limit in being able to deal with that. And people across the road and in other flats shouted right back at him, and for about half an hour everyone was just shouting at everyone and it was all weirdly cathartic. And then the police arrived with sirens and a loudhailer and shouted even louder, just in case anyone had still been asleep.

Any moment now had been the catchphrase of that first week. And, after that, *Any day now*. Because Harry understood narrative. He understood that you don't go visit the magic land and get told that you're the heir to the throne and make your daring escape from the monsters and then just… sit on your hands for a week. For *two* weeks, by then. Just… making lonely masked trips to the off licence and the miniature supermarket and the corner shop. Answering the door to find the package already abandoned there and the delivery driver fleeing down the stairs. Gone so thoroughly the fairies might have brought it. Moving through depopulated streets and even those people he met keeping clear of him, passing without a glance or a word as though each was in their own closed and separate world.

In the third week, Harry was forced to admit that he probably hadn't been to Underhill. It didn't seem likely, compared to the odds of a psychotic break given all the family history-related stress he'd been under. He called his therapist, who of course wasn't taking visitors. Eventually there was an awkward Zoom session which did very little for Harry except bring to him just how reliant he was on all the regular human cues and tics of other people to maintain a basic conversation. He could see the therapist. He could hear her voice, slightly out of sync with her lips. And… nothing. A void where the human contact was supposed to be.

He told her everything. He told it like someone narrating a story, peppering the narrative with disclaimers and doubts, but he told her. *I (obviously didn't, but work with me here) went into a wardrobe (and I know that's the other stories, not...) into (what seemed to be very real at the time) a magic land.* And the therapist nodded and made notes and asked him if he was feeling as though he might harm himself or anyone else. And Harry didn't mention the knife and said no, he didn't think so. He was more worried about being harmed by all the (plainly imaginary) things from the magic land he had (obviously not really) been to. And she said in that case there wasn't much she could do, but she'd write to his local GP to prompt a new and more potent prescription and maybe that would help. And he'd said, "I don't think you understand. I somehow lost a month of my time whilst spending a day or so lost in a fictional country," and she said, "Seriously, right now, what do you expect me to do about that?" Asking rather plaintively as though *he* had taken the therapist hat for a moment and had all the answers.

He dreamt of Underhill. He didn't want to. They weren't good dreams. It wasn't the green and radiant land of the books. It was just as he remembered, all coming apart. The constant filter of the non-snow, like particles of dead matter falling to the sea floor for the worms and the crabs to pick over. The hollow, corroded pylons of the trees. All the characters from the books slowly decaying, eaten away from within by the cancer that was time. Intended to be the playmates of intrepid children and now left over, unwanted, desperate for... something. And he suffered, and woke sweating, convinced every morning he'd come down with the *thing* that was gripping the world around him in its own version of decaying winter. The land was sick, ergo so was the king, surely. A dolorous stroke that cut both ways.

One night he looked out of the window and saw the faun there, or thought he did. Timon, in his shabby coat, standing out in the alley with the bins. Just staring. Horrible, wrong-legged, horned. The streetlight turned his flaking, pockmarked skin a cancerous yellow. And Harry felt a jolt of fear and went and got the knife. And when he returned, Timon was gone. In his wake was a weird disappointment. *I guess I'm not that important after all.* Maybe they had a whole list of potential heirs. Maybe the magic kingdom had given up on Felix 'Harry' Bodie.

Any day now turned into *Soon* and then to *Perhaps*. And he understood that something had happened that never did, in those stories. He'd missed his chance. He'd had that one shot at the magical land and it had been horrible, so he'd rejected it. And rather than bounding after him like an enthusiastic puppy, the magic had just shrugged and written him off. Moved on, or just settled down to die, or declared a republic and done away with all that kings and bloodlines nonsense. Some solution that didn't involve him.

And he went and got groceries, and ordered take-out from the three places still open. He tried to connect virtually with people he wouldn't really have had much to say to physically, finding the screen between them more of a barrier than the gap between realities. He had awkward calls with his agent and a handful of acting acquaintances, and none of it fed that part of him that needed to be human.

And eventually he called Seitchman. Because by then his stir-craziness was turning into a different kind of craziness. He felt he'd missed a clue. Obviously, it couldn't all just have been for nothing. He was like a character in a computer game who hadn't noticed the big gold exclamation mark over someone's head, and was now just wandering about lost because they hadn't picked up the right quest. And because there was no useful online wiki for 'Felix Bodie's Delusions' he could look stuff up in, and he didn't fancy tracking down the Underlings, that left only the private investigator.

"Hello?" Her voice curious, no introduction, no 'private investigator for hire' tacked on to the end.

"Seitchman?" He couldn't remember her forename.

"Hello?" after a pause; wary.

"It's Bodie. Felix Bodie."

More pause.

"Harry. It's Harry."

Even as he repeated the name, he heard the sudden intake of breath. "*Harry?* Fuck, it *is* you. Where are you?"

"I'm... at home." A weirdly deflating answer given the urgency of the question. "I..."

"I thought... I didn't know what I thought." Her words tripped over themselves to get out. "What *happened?*"

"I..." Feeling himself at the brink of a conversational abyss. And he could pull back. He could lie—or alternatively tell the most likely objective truth despite the things he personally remembered experiencing. But then what would be the point of the call?

And his courage failed him and instead he said, "I want to hire you."

A pause of a different character, more baffled than wary now, punctuated at last by, "…Huh?"

"To investigate," Harry told her. He didn't—this was pure invention on his part—but he was talking with another human being and suddenly he didn't want to let go of it. Even though it was a near-stranger. Even though it was someone who'd got him into so much shit.

"Mr Bodie, where the hell have you *been?* I texted you, like, a thousand times."

"I didn't get them," he told her. "I…" Abruptly his conversational feet slipped. "I was there. Underhill."

He braced. A third distinct pause intruded into the call and he was terrified she'd hang up. "Look, you don't have to believe me—"

"I saw you walk into a wardrobe and vanish," she told him flatly. "You just receded away from me like there was infinite space. And just… *gone.*"

"What were you expecting?" he got out.

"I—" She actually coughed. "My client said there might be a reaction."

"There was a fucking reaction."

"Yeah, I got that. Right. You need me to get you back to the wardrobe?"

"I…" *Do I?* "I mean, that's not an option, and anyway…" *Would I, if I could?* Because that was why he'd called her, surely. She was the hair-thin thread linking him to *that place*, or at least the thread that wouldn't turn up some kind of murderer or monster if he tugged on it. And it had been horrible in Underhill. Obviously he didn't want to *go* there again. Except... it was pretty horrible here in London, England, right now, and at least in Underhill people had been pleased to see him. Getting weirdly nostalgic for 'that time I sat with a decaying faun in the non-snow and just talked' was the saddest thing he'd ever conceived, but that didn't mean it wasn't true. "The wardrobe got trashed when I came out," he explained. Wondering if, otherwise, he'd be haunting the street outside that Oxfordshire house like Timon in the alley. "I... need you to investigate someone who's been hanging round my flat." *Who has horns and hooves and kills people*. But he couldn't say that.

"That right?" Seitchman said at last.

"Someone who's... involved." *Really quite heavily involved. As in 'he comes from an imaginary fairyland' involved.*

"You got any details on this 'someone,' or can I just pick my own?" she asked him eventually, and he realised that, while his head was thronging with information, he hadn't actually told her anything.

"Yes, he's..." Again that brink. Even with the previous admission, he couldn't tell a private detective 'I want you to track down a mythological entity, please.' And it wasn't as if he had much to go on. Short of asking Seitchman to stake out his flat and hope Timon made a showing, what was there? "You know what? Never mind. Stupid idea."

"Tall fellow, long coat?" she prompted. "Walks funny."

It was Harry's turn with the interesting silence.

"Only someone answering to that description showed up skulking near the—near the office. And someone broke the window of my car and went through my glove box. And it seemed to me that might just be life, or it might be connected with the case. And so I've been doing some digging already." And despite the whole professional investigator angle, he could hear a slight shake to her voice. *Who investigates the investigators?*

"You saw him."

"At a safe distance. I followed him two nights ago. A long way. Likes his constitutional."

"You've been *spying* on him?"

"You were gone. I didn't have any other leads."

"Seitchman, he *killed* two of the Underlings."

More silence, and then, "Welp. Didn't know that."

"Where did he go?"

"A bar."

"What?"

"A bar," she repeated. "I mean yes, supposed to be closed, all that. Just beer bottle takeaways right now. Except it doesn't really take a PI to work out there's a backroom that's still catering to a select clientele. And it's a pretty weirdass bar to begin with. Let's just say, one where suddenly having to wear a mask didn't massively inconvenience anyone."

"Meaning what?" Harry asked. *Where the hell can something like Timon hide, precisely?*

Seitchman snorted. "You know what a *furry* is, Mr Bodie?"

*　　*　　*

SHE HAD A phone number for the bar. He could ask her to go back there, but he thought about Warrington and Thistlesham, and how Timon might react to a third party nosing into Underhill business. Instead, *he* somehow ended up working for *Seitchman*, promising he'd call the bar himself and let her know what he turned up.

What he turned up was a recorded message saying that Teddy's was closed except for takeaways and cautioning all its regular clientele to take care and social distance, which Harry found oddly touching. He did get to record his own stammering rejoinder, in which he said he was Felix and left a message so that he could be contacted by... he almost said 'Tim,' to maintain some ludicrous cover, but went with 'Timon' because, really, who was he kidding? Any party who got hold of the message would either already know what was going on, or never be able to penetrate the mystery.

A day later, he got a call back. Typically, he was expecting his agent, the whole Underhill business briefly out of his head. The watchful near-quiet after he answered threw him. He could hear the distant beat of music, he thought, and ragged breathing.

"Hello?" he pressed, and a hoarse voice said, "My prince...?"

Timon. The faun on the phone.

"Right," Harry said, his own voice catching. "Listen. I'm talking and you're listening." Pause; no objection, so apparently his conditions had been accepted. "I'm not promising anything, right? I just… It happened. I was *there*. I can't… ignore it. I just want to talk." And of course he *was* talking, but that wasn't what he meant. Not second hand over the phone. Not distanced, socially or otherwise. "I don't know what you want, and I don't know what *I* want, but… I tried to make it all just be in my head, but I'm not even the only person who's seen you. I vanished into a wardrobe before someone's eyes. Something *real* is going on."

"Yes," said Timon quietly. "I am real." Which was exactly what a figment of his imagination would say, but Seitchman's involvement meant either everything *was* real or the PI was magnificently reverse-gaslighting him.

"I'm going to come and talk to you. I'm bringing backup." The words bobbed to his tongue from that police drama he'd guested on once. "You're going to tell me what's going on and what all those…"—he almost said 'clowns,' but there had only been one clown and Harry didn't want to think about *him*—"*people* want with me."

"And then?" Timon's voice had a terrible hunger to it.

"And nothing. Just talk," Harry insisted. Knowing that there might be a room full of monster clowns and spiders waiting for him, but also knowing that he *had* to get a handle on this thing that had been stabbed into his life, and where else could he turn?

Timon's home was a charming little house in a glade in the woods, dug into the side of a hill. He had little round windows and an oval door on one hinge, and he had trained flowers to grow up the sides in bursts of red and blue and purple. Inside was as light and airy as could be wished, and there was always more space than you expected. When guests came to call, no matter how many, he could always find room for everyone without his living room becoming crowded, and his pantry never ran short of food or drink...

The Nine Stones of Underhill (1953),
Mary Bodie, Targamane Press

CHAPTER SEVEN

Seitchman met him outside Teddy's, which had a black-painted pub front with darkened windows, and must have looked closed even when fully open. She looked shifty, or at least shiftier than normal. Her hands were in her coat pockets again, and he wondered if, this time, there really was a gun.

"You let me do the talking," he told her, and she nodded, then brought her hand out. He flinched, but it was just her phone.

"I'll record everything," she explained, through her mask. "For your client."

A beat. "Right, yes." So patently false he almost called her on it. He needed a unified front, though. He was, after all, a children's entertainer with ambitions to one day playing a madman. She was a woman of action, a hard-bitten private eye.

"I don't suppose," he said, after the two of them had loitered around the front of Teddy's without either of them actually taking any step towards going in, "you actually have a gun?"

"Why would I have a gun?"

"Because you're a private eye."

"Ah." Another glaringly awkward beat. "You've watched too many movies." Another beat. "Actual dead people, huh?"

Apparently Seitchman hadn't been bitten as hard as he'd thought. "Two Underlings. A retired judge and a banker. Nothing someone in your line of work can't handle."

"Fuck," Seitchman muttered. She looked up and down the grimy little street as though somehow someone might overhear them. "Okay, Bodie, I'm going to come clean with you now."

"There's no client," he filled in for her.

"There is no client," she agreed. "I'm also not a private eye."

"I knew it—wait, what?"

"I'm a folklorist."

"A what?" He had taken a step away from her, aware that his voice was rising, even through the mask. "I mean, what even is that?"

"I study folklore. I'm a doctor of it. Doctor Rebecca Seitchman. If that helps."

"How could that possibly help? Wait, is this that...?" He couldn't remember the name. "Karen? Karen Svoboda? The wizard guy?" The image of a man in a pointy hat demanding to see the manager flickered briefly in his mind.

It took Seitchman a moment to catch on. "Carolus

Svoboda? Kind of. But mostly I specialise in accounts of visiting Faerie and similar otherworlds. Which kind of drifted into academic analysis of portal fiction, because that opens up a whole extra bucket of potential funding from the lit crowd. Which led me to Underhill, the Underlings, the whole weird underground thread about it being *real*."

"I have lived under the shadow of those books since I was born," Harry pointed out. "Nobody ever suggested to *me* any of it was real. Up until Timon the goddamned faun turned up in the garden."

She shrugged. "I'm guessing you didn't spend several hundred hours in academic research of the topic. Are we going in or what?"

THERE WAS ONE disconsolate-looking bear-costumed patron inside Teddy's. They were not, Harry considered, having a picnic. Staring at the slightly tatty animal onesie gave him the shudders, and a moment later he had to hold back a fit of giggles. *Nature is healing*, he thought helplessly.

The man behind the bar, just coming out to hand the bear a plastic bag of clunking cans, wore a more conventional style of mask. He peered at Harry and Seitchman, narrow eyed, as though they hadn't made the dress code. At last he asked, "You Bodie?"

"I am, yes."

A quick scan through the shaded windows revealed no police around to enforce lockdown laws. "In the back," said the barman, and Harry's thousand questions—starting with *Just where the hell do you fit into all this?*—died stillborn. Did the man think Timon's appearance was just elaborate makeup and costume? Was he a closet *Underhill* fan whose dreams had come true? The man's suspicious gaze warded off all enquiry, as did the black cloth mask itself. The pandemic had turned everyone into vigilantes and highwaymen, too dangerous to question.

On the phone, he hadn't said to Timon, 'Come alone.' He hadn't thought he'd need to. And so Timon wasn't alone. The capacious, windowless back room of Teddy's had a complement of three.

Harry stopped so hard that Seitchman ran into him. And no, it wasn't *them:* no Hulder, no Wish Dog, no Gombles, thank God. As well as the faun's gaunt shape there was a dwarfish creature at one round table who wore a hooded cloak and had the clawed feet of a bird, and the sagging rodent thing keeping a pointed distance from it was probably not just someone small in a fur suit. He could vaguely identify both from the books, if he cared to think back. Not as individuals, but as representatives of some monster-of-the-week adversary seen off by James and Jemima without too much trouble. He felt both of them staring at him every time he wasn't looking, but they buried their snouts in their beer the moment he tried to catch their gaze.

Timon was hunched at a corner table. He watched the pair of them come over, eyes flicking from Harry to Seitchman.

"You," he noted.

She stopped a few paces clear of taking up a chair. "Right." Doubtless thinking of the murders.

Timon sent Harry an aggrieved look, but this time Harry wasn't having any of it.

"Without her I wouldn't even have this place's number. Now are you going to talk or what? She's going to record it all. She's going to send me a copy—right? That way I can listen back to it and know that I'm not going totally crazy. Or are you going to tell me your voice will magically not turn up on a recording or something?"

"I'm right here," said Seitchman in a small voice. "I'm seeing him too. With the horns and everything."

"For all I know I could be imagining you too," Harry told her harshly. "You're a folklorist pretending to be a PI pretending to be a lawyer. That's marginally less plausible than an actual *faun*."

"Then how would having a recording help, precisely?" she asked.

"Just..." Harry realised he was shaking. That he was about to burst into tears like a small child. All the tension that had been ratcheting up since *How Even Me?* was catching up on him, not helped at all by the encounters with Timon and the cloak-and-dagger with Seitchman; by the kidnap and murder; by the real-world isolation; by actually goddamn *travelling to Underhill*. None of it had gone anywhere. He'd been denied any kind of escape valve, and now either he let some of it out or he was going to snap.

And Timon seemed to understand that. "Just sit down," he invited them both. "Sit and we'll talk, just like you said. What do you want to know?"

"I..." Harry dropped into a chair, staring across the scored table at the skewbald, unwell-looking creature. There was a touch of ultraviolet in the back room's lighting, and the flaking, fungous patches on Timon's skin glowed as though his life-force was seeping out of them. "I just want to know... *what?* I want to know, *What, even?* Just... *what?*" No way of even beginning a cogent question.

Seitchman warily took the chair next to him, shifting it sideways for a bit of extra space.

"What do you want?" Harry finally got out, hearing his voice ragged with emotion. "Any of you. All of you." *Why can't you leave me alone?* Except he'd had that chance, and he'd picked at the scab anyway. It was he who'd come to beard Timon in the faun's den. And had Underhill been the green and innocent place of the books, maybe that would make sense. Maybe that justified the yearning of the Underlings, the other people who thought they'd encountered something real from the fiction. Who maybe *had* encountered it, given who he was sitting across from. But when he'd gone to Underhill it had been horrible and dying, and *still* he'd come back. Because it was there. Because he meant something there, even though he didn't know what.

"I don't know what *I* want," Timon said carefully, "but the *Queen* wants you back. That's who Wish Dog was fetching you for."

"The Queen?" Harry blinked. In the books, James and Jemima were nominally the rulers of Underhill whenever they were there, as apparently being human outranked anything else and the place had never heard of participatory democracy. There'd been no mention of a queen, unless fictional Jemima was somehow clinging on.

"You surfaced just in time, really," Timon said mournfully. "The land had lost track of you entirely. We don't... understand a lot of what you've got over here, those of us who've crept out over the years. But they have daytime TV in the bar, and there you were, talking about being the heir of the kingdom. And so I slipped back and told them. And then you came to us. Just as everyone hoped. It was like everything was waking up again, just for a moment. And then you left."

"What...?" Harry ordered his thoughts. "What's wrong with the place? I mean, all that white stuff, the..." An abortive gesture at the faun's own peeling face. "You know, not like it is in the books."

"It's *old*, Harry," said Timon. "Long past its use-by date. We've been waiting for a long time. And *she*'s old, too. I mean, my advice to you, you want rid of us? Just stay away. Give it another five years, fifteen at most. We'll be gone. Just your grandmother's books left. Probably for the best." He stared at his flaking hands.

"Why?"

"Because the land is the queen and the queen is the land," Seitchman put in. "You know how it goes. The king receives a wound, so the land is wounded. All that Arthurian stuff. And the Queen of Underhill is old, so..."

"What queen, though?" Harry pressed. Timon gave him an incredulous look.

"Seriously? You haven't worked that one out? She'd be your, what, great-great-grandmother."

Harry blinked. He had a feeling this was a crashing revelation only to him.

"The blood descendant of Carolus Svoboda, mother of Devaty Svoboda, who was mother of Magda Bodie, a.k.a. Mary," Seitchman filled in helpfully, for the benefit of her phone. "The royal line of Underhill. Apparently. This health thing, not just a metaphor then?"

Timon gave her a wry look. "Ask him. He's seen it."

"My great-great-grandmother's *alive?*" Harry hissed.

Timon shrugged. "I mean, just. I mean, not for long. Clinging on, like all of us. And it's like that show you had ages ago, with the dead cat. When she goes to eternal sleep, all her subjects go too..."

"And she wants me for..."

"To hand the kingdom over, maybe." Timon shrugged.

"You don't seem very invested in it, given it's supposedly your continued existence too," Seitchman noted.

Timon just looked at her. A faun who walked into a bar. *Why the long face?* "Hulder thinks we should just let go," he observed, a partial sequitur at best. "It's not much of a life, after all. And some of us have started making... alternative arrangements." A gesture around the back room and its two other occupants.

"But..." Harry felt weirdly as though he had a duty to defend the world he'd read about in the books. "But the adventures, all those things you did with James and Jemima, wasn't that... fun?"

The faun's expression was withering. "Those were just books, Harry. You know, *fiction.*"

That seemed a particularly unfair card for the fictional creature to play.

"But…"

"It was supposed to go that way," Timon went on slowly. "That was what we were *for*, after all. But then your great-grandmother got out, after putting all that work in, and took your grandmother with her. You know, the girl it was all in aid of."

"What?"

"So there we were," the faun said, "all ready to have adventures and battles and escapades and, you know, *fun*. Except the child was born over here; in a mental hospital, apparently. And instead of living in Underhill and *going* on those adventures, she just heard about it all second hand from her mother, and turned it into a series of books. While we waited and waited, and she never came to visit. And nor did her daughter. And, until very recently, nor did you."

"You want me," Harry got out, "to come and have *adventures* with you?"

"No," the faun said, somewhat too firmly in Harry's opinion, as though Harry had already failed the adventurer application at interview stage. "The Queen and Wish Dog want you to come and breathe new life into the world so that things can go on. And Hulder and some others don't want you to do that. And I don't know what I want, but worst comes to worst I'll live here as an undocumented immigrant and just have to wear a hat all the time."

Harry found he was gripping the table, unwilling to even

look at Seitchman in case that much grounding in reality was fatal. "And what about what *I* want?"

"And what do you want?" Timon asked him.

"What if I want to do it?" Waiting for Seitchman's warning tones, which didn't come. He could sense her watching him, waiting for which way he'd jump. "What if I want to go back to Underhill." *Back to the old country. My inheritance. Family!* Somewhere he would actually be important and mean something. Not the fool after all, but the king. Because he'd trashed the wardrobe, but that hadn't stopped Timon hopping in and out of Underhill since. The faun and these other refugees had a railroad out of fairyland.

"Bodie," Seitchman said.

"Don't try to stop me." Because if she did, he'd cave. He had that little resolution in him.

"I want to come too," she told him fiercely. "I want to see it. I mean, he's right," she added direct to Timon. "Obviously you've got a two-way door somewhere."

The faun looked between them. Harry couldn't tell if the melancholy was an act or not. "You're not going to like it," he said. "You've both read the books, right? You know who it is, who's always coming out of dark corners and holes, just popping up wherever she's not wanted. Part of the skillset she was designed for,"

Harry and Seitchman exchanged looks, and then Timon recited, in an unpleasant singsong voice, "*But even though the naughty faun had locked every door three times and thrown all the bolts, still* she *found a crack to creep in, squeezing her bloated body almost flat until she had wriggled her way out of the cell and gone scuttling away to lick her wounds.* And she does. She finds every crack. Even if it's a crack between one world and another. We're very grateful for her." He gave a broken little chuckle. "I remember when she was a monster. But it's been a long time, waiting for the true heir of Underhill. You get used to people. You rub along. Even with Smackersnack. Especially with her, in these latter days."

"Smackersnack," Harry echoed. "The spider. The *spider* can get out of Underhill."

"With passengers," Timon agreed. "And back in. With passengers. It's quick and easy getting in, though the return journey takes a while. Longer and longer, the more things decay back there. You must have noticed."

"And you can, what, go get her? Have her come and drive the bus back to Underhill?" Seitchman asked him.

Timon gave her a look. "Well, I don't need to, do I? She's in the next room, listening to all this, right now."

The castle, as always when James and Jemima came back from their adventures, had prepared a grand feast to welcome their return. There was fresh bread, toasted, with butter melting on it, bowls of crisp apples, slices of ham and cheese, and hard-boiled eggs. There were little chocolate cakes and almond cakes and cakes with strawberry jam, and to drink they had hot possets steaming with nutmeg...

The Horns of Underhill (1954),
Mary Bodie, Targamane Press

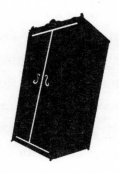

CHAPTER EIGHT

IF SEITCHMAN HADN'T been there, then Harry would probably just have called it a day, backed out of Teddy's with apologies, bought an armful of beer bottles and gone to drink himself into a stupor. Seitchman hadn't seen the spider, though, and she was full of questions.

"She's the only one who can go in and out?" and, "How long's she been doing it?" and, "Isn't she supposed to be one of the villains?" until Timon held up his hands and said, "You may as well just talk to her." And it was more than Harry could do to duck out under Seitchman's keen gaze. Letting himself down was second nature, but introduce someone else into the mix and there were expectations to live up to.

And in the next room, indeed, was Smackersnack, the spider.

It was a cellar, of course. There were still barrels and boxes along one wall, the bar's shrivelled stock. The other wall was... a giant spider's home office, was the only way Harry could characterise it. It was swathed and sheeted with filthy, ragged webbing until all sense of the hard boundaries of walls and ceiling and floor were entirely lost. And in the midst of that, hanging head down and filling much of the space, there she was. With her laptop.

Harry took a while to digest that. And this obviously wasn't some verminous infestation the bar owner just hadn't got around to clearing out yet. Someone had run a set of cables down here, for a start. They emerged from the web, twined with errant silk, to plug into the laptop's ports. The radiance of the screen glimmered back from the depths of Smackersnack's plate-sized eyes as her smaller mouthparts tapped away at the keyboard and touchpad.

"Responding to your rudeness," came her soft, whispery voice, "we were intended for antagonism indeed. Absence of opportunity led to looking for other options. They created me for creeping and crawling. I picked up the paths of my precursor and perfected them."

Seitchman had stopped dead at the sight of the monster, but the voice seemed to have flipped some mental toggle in her, from *thing* to *person*. She approached far closer than Harry was happy to, staring at the gigantic arachnid. "By 'precursor' you mean... the rulers of Underhill. Harry's family. They can come and go, can't they?"

"The crown cherishes that capability," Smackersnack agreed. Her attention finally left the screen to goggle at her visitors. "Hello, Harry," she said. "And curious companion."

"Why help others get out of Underhill?" Seitchman asked her.

The spider shifted, ropes of webbing pulling taut and sagging as her weight moved. Those fangs, every bit as huge and barbed as Harry had feared, flexed a little. *Jesus god, don't offend it!*

"This world wants no wicked webbers," Smackersnack said. "Human hands are helpful. Under obligation."

"Timon and company can go places you can't, right?" Seitchman tried to peer at the laptop but the spider tilted it away from her jealously. "Surfing the web, is it?"

"We stream," the spider said, deadpan. "Without webcam."

Harry broke in. "If I wanted to get back. Back to Underhill. If I wanted to meet my great—my ancestress. And maybe fix things. If they can be fixed. If I wanted to do my *duty*, by my family. Could you get me back there?" His voice trembled as the spider's attention shifted to him.

"Easy as eyeblinks," said the creature that, presumably, couldn't actually blink. "Everyone's aware, Smackersnack sneaks everywhere." An actual line from one of the books, and Harry wondered dizzily if the spider, and other Underhill characters, read about their own supposed adventures.

"Are you sure about this, Harry?" Seitchman asked.

No, absolutely not. Get me out of here. I'm about to do something stupid. But his mouth said, "Yes." And then, "You're taking this very well."

Seitchman looked as though she was going to say something very private eye-y and just shrug it off, but then she glanced from Timon to the huge spider and just nodded.

"I am. I really am. I always felt that if I found something

genuinely uncanny I'd run screaming, but apparently not. Which is just as well because I want to go. All the way to Underhill."

Harry knew it was entirely for her own reasons, as some sort of maverick folklorist—or whatever she actually was—but the wash of relief almost reduced him to tears. "God, yes," he told her. When he looked back to the spider, Smackersnack had silently come two striding steps closer. He saw himself reflected in her eyes.

"Fearful thoughts, faun," she said. "To rescue the realm or let it rot? You told us you'd turned your back on the birthplace. Exile instead. A home here with the humans."

Timon looked away, one hand coming up to finger the ridges of his horns. Harry wondered how much he had managed to feign the human, even a little. Had he just wandered, one more homeless denizen of London that people hurried past and didn't look too closely at? Or maybe that was just Harry's own knee-jerk hot take. Maybe Timon was another industrious, hard-working immigrant, shoring up the city economy.

"Do it," the faun said. "Take us through."

THERE WAS NONE of the yawning timeless moment Harry had felt on exiting Underhill. The long stuck instant that had translated into so much lost time back in what he stubbornly thought of as the real world. There was also no being wrapped in cocoons by the spider as part of the transit process, for which he was profoundly grateful.

Smackersnack just fussed with the hanging folds of her web until she had identified some specific point she could tear open, and there, where there should have been the plasterboard of the cellar wall, was the drifted non-snow and stark black forest of Underhill-as-it-now-was. And, when he, Seitchman and Timon had stepped through, the spider squeezed her bulk after them and then closed up the yawning hole in a sheet of grimy webbing strung between two trunks. And that was it; they were in Underhill.

"Fuck," Seitchman said reverently. She had her arms hugged about herself. "Damn, it's cold."

"It's the energy exchange," said Smackersnack. Words as odd as Timon mentioning 'scaling problems' with regard to the outsized clown. "Easy to enter, down the decline. Underhill's empty, after all. Your wonderful world is bursting with busyness, though. Hard to haul hand over hand up the incline. Takes time."

"In some stories, when someone visits fairyland, they come out years, decades, even centuries later," Seitchman whispered. "You know, Brigadoon, a day in the otherworld is a lifetime in ours. Except maybe it's not the time spent there. It's the transit. An energy gradient. Because this place certainly seems less energetic, wouldn't you say?"

"I don't think you're meant to think about magic kingdoms in terms of the physics," Harry told her, feeling oddly proprietorial. After all, he was the heir to it all and he didn't want people doing science to his birthright.

From somewhere far off—yet still far too close—he heard the hooting, honking cry of Gombles.

"Oh, damn," he said. "Is everything going to know where I am again?"

Timon nodded gloomily.

"Will you take me to the castle?"

"You're sure, are you?"

Harry gave the faun an exasperated look. "Will you give me any kind of straight answer if I ask you why I shouldn't be?"

Timon's face just got longer and he shuffled his hooves in the non-snow. "It's complicated," he said at last. "I did all I could. Found a way out. Found you. I tried to make everyone happy. That's what they made me to do. I can't make the decision, Harry. I was only ever meant to be a supporting character. I can't tell what's right. I never could." The mischievous faun, always getting into scrapes. A good heart, but a troublemaker. That rascally Timon. Only he'd grown old, like some stoner student friend who still hasn't got it together in his late forties.

Smackersnack shifted her weight from leg to leg, waiting.

"Just take me," Harry decided. "I want to meet the Queen. I want to claim my birthright."

THEY HAD TO practically drag Seitchman along, because she wanted to look at *everything*. Once she even tried to climb one of the trees. She got quite high before a branch just disintegrated under her and she was dumped unceremoniously in the non-snow mounded at its base.

"It's all broken up there," she explained thoughtfully.

"Just… stumps of branches, scaffolding. The whole place is like one of those abandoned amusement parks. It's all fake."

"It's just run down," Harry decided. "But it's going to get better."

She gave him an odd look. "Because you're here, right?"

"You heard them." And he didn't know if he believed any of it, but he *wanted* to. He so dearly wanted to. Because he could fix this. He couldn't fix his own world and he couldn't fix his sad shambles of a life, but here was a magic kingdom that just needed the heir to return to restore it to glorious blooming summer, apparently. And he was the heir, and he'd returned. He knew how the story went, and aside from having the right provenance, there wasn't much else it required from him. Even he couldn't fuck this one up.

The others found them soon enough, winding their way uphill between the trees, towards that unseen castle. Hulder first, stepping gracefully out into their path, staring at Harry with wide, sad eyes. And soon after she fell into step, there was Wish Dog, panting eagerly, as huge and horrible as Harry remembered. And yet pathetic, desperate. Just a dog who wanted to be scratched behind the one decaying ear he still had. He growled at Smackersnack, and she lifted her legs and hissed at him, but it was just for show. A motheaten old circus act.

And the mourning, bellowing hoots followed them, from behind, echoing in their wake, but they kept up their pace and Gombles never caught them. And then there was the castle.

The trees gave out without warning, and the pallid luminescence of the not-snow crawled up the tumbled stones of fallen walls. It filtered past them like the last invading army to touch the bases of towers that tottered up into the absolute darkness of the sky, punched with ragged holes where windows had decayed outwards like rotten teeth. And, half-lost in that leaching glimmer, Harry saw another light. A warmer light, though marginally. The faintest of flickering amber glows from inside. They had reached the heart of Underhill, and someone was at home.

There was a wretched straggle of creatures within the circle of those tumbled walls, but their names weren't on the list for entrance, apparently. They were all different shapes and sizes, shrouded in multiple layers of cloth long-faded from once-cheery colours. Some were unfamiliar, others he recognised vaguely. Side-characters and types, background fodder. The good folk of Underhill, to be saved by the gallant James and Jemima without ever getting any real say in it. And now they were limping and shambling up, and within their cowls were beaks and muzzles and whispers and glassy eyes like a taxidermist's miscellany drawer. They whispered and pointed and stared. Wish Dog's growl sent them tumbling cravenly back and then the little band was past the sagging stone arch and within the castle proper.

The light came from—

"Oh, that's nasty," Seitchman said, and Harry could only agree. How had the great castle of Underhill been illuminated in the books? The detail had never come up. It had always been clear-skied day in Underhill, after all. Certainly his grandmother had never penned the detail *live fireflies the size of someone's head, nailed to the walls, writhing and twitching as they gave out an amber radiance.* The actual quality of the light was eerily like the streetlamps outside his flat.

There were *things* inside the castle. They looked like tangled dust bunnies that came up to Harry's chest level, knots of grey fibres and loose ends bundled about a crude skeleton of sticks. Their eyes were mirror shards. They approached with jerky stop-motion speed and started plucking mutely at Harry's clothes. Sharp-fingered hands reached, flinched back, reached again. He saw fragments of twig and stone repurposed as skeleton, bunched cords and fibres wrapped around them as musculature. The bare minimum to make a moving manikin.

"These things weren't in the books," Seitchman said. "What are they?"

"After things had fallen apart enough," Hulder said softly, "and the kingdom wasn't functioning, *she* had to make them. To do, for her. Even though it cost us a lot of what we had. They are... she called them *robota*."

"Cree-py-3PO," Harry muttered, shaking off a clicking hand. And then the little eddy of dust bunny things had ushered them into a great, ruinous hall and there she was, seated at the far end of a long table he remembered from the books. They had great celebrations here, he recalled. Lovingly described food-based reward-fests drawn straight from the post-war scarcity Granma Magda had lived through. James and Jemima had been cheered for whatever threat-of-the-week they'd saved the kingdom from, before their seamless return to their rather dull lives in the real world. And in precisely none of those scenes had there been someone at the head of the table other than the two vacuous protagonists.

She was very old. If she was who Timon said, then she was older than people really got, and looked it. She was as pallid white as the non-snow, and he could see how her skin had fallen to wrinkles over the years, and then pulled into taut, leathery creases after that. If she hadn't been moving, he'd have taken her for the sort of withered corpse that got pulled out of bogs with a rope around its neck.

Her hair, the yellow-white of old bone, was piled high on her head in the remains of an elaborate coiffure. She wore what had once been a magnificent gown, all lace and gold, broad ballooning skirt, rows of pearls. It had faded, and parts of it had gone threadbare or just detached, inner layers shown like a cutaway diagram or a time-lapse of decay. Everything about her was dust and faded glory. As though someone had been cosplaying Marie Antoinette, and then died, and then been left somewhere mostly dry for quite a long time. And then woken up.

The eyes were like milky marbles, but he saw them roll and move in their sockets, and one emaciated hand indicated the rows of chairs. Wish Dog trotted over and sat on his haunches beside her, radiating *I'm a good boy* except for all the exposed teeth and missing fur.

The voice that issued from those raisin lips was like the snapping of twigs, twisted with the dregs of an accent Harry couldn't place.

"Now we are all gathered," said his great-great-grandmother. "We shall have a feast."

They sat, leaving a good few empty chairs between anyone and the head of the table. Harry and Seitchman, Timon and Hulder. A handful of other Underhill creatures too: a humanoid cat called Trumpy; a big-eared gnome character that was either Punko or Pinko, neither of which names had really come over as Granma had intended to a later generation of readers; some other little capering thing which probably had a name, but Harry couldn't place it for the fair reason that its face had fallen off at some time in the interim, leaving just a ragged-edged hole. It made a hollow gulping noise at him, and he looked away hurriedly. Smackersnack had found refuge up where one wall met the bowed health and safety hazard of the ceiling.

A procession of the fibrous dust bunnies marched in, bearing platters and tureens and bowls, and began to set out what would have been a creditable feast had any of it contained any kind of food. Mostly what it contained was dust, but some vessels still had a film of dried nastiness inside them. Some royal cook had prepared this magnificent repast for the triumphal return of the heir, perhaps, and then left it set out in the kitchens for the next several generations until Harry finally arrived to take up the mantle.

His hands shook as a tarnished silver plate was set before him. There were a handful of withered things on it that looked like ten year-dead fingers. He didn't ask about them. He sent no compliments to the chef.

From beyond the walls, he heard the mournful cry of

Gombles, and for once he felt the forlorn clown had hit the nail on the head.

But I'm back now. New life into the world. Everything gets better from here. That's the point of me. It's nice to have a point.

"So you are the child of my child," came the oddly canted voice of his ancestress.

"With a few more generations thrown in," Harry agreed, and then yelped because one of the dust bunnies had stabbed him. He stared at the thing, and at the blood glistening on the tip of one claw finger. Its mirror-shard eyes showed him his aghast expression before it hurried off.

"We shall see," the ancient woman wheezed, "if you are suitable. We shall analyse you, in our laboratory. To see if you are within tolerance."

Harry blinked. "To save Underhill," he pressed. "To stop this place dying, right?"

"Yes," she breathed, and he felt an absurd spike of happiness, despite everything.

"I never knew," he said softly. "I'd have come sooner. But there were only the books."

"Yes, the books," broke in Seitchman. "Excuse me, Your Highness, but I have a few questions. Doctor Rebecca Seitchman, folklorist, associate at Somerville College, Oxford. Specialist in folk traditions as they're reinvented in children's lit. How come this place is set up as a kid's story, precisely?"

Harry turned to her. "Seitchman, this is the original. The books came later."

"No, really," she said. "The faun even said he was just a *supporting character*. This is not set up like a traditional fairy tale, let alone any place real."

"My grandmother never saw this place," Harry insisted, aware of the dry gaze of his ancestress on him. "She just had the stories from *her* mother, which she turned into the books. But this is…"

"Pretty much exactly that place, except that the events of the stories never happened. And neither did anything else. And it's sat here for a long time and just decayed while all the little critters basically tried to keep skin and bone together. And mostly failed at that. Your Highness, how *old* is Underhill? Earth years?"

The ancestress leant forwards in creaky stages, blind eyes fixed on the folklorist. "We made it for the child, she and I," she whispered. "You're very perspicacious, Doctor Seitchman. A scientific philosopher perhaps?"

"Folklorist," Seitchman said defiantly, with the air of someone who had to defend their field of study on the regular.

The withered visage pursed into a face that, in other circumstances, would have been turning down a departmental funding application. "Unfortunate. I prefer those who study the universe ab ovo rather than from hearsay testimony. Einstein, such a mind!" A scratchy little chuckle. "You believe you have questions."

"I always do." Seitchman sounded shaken but determined. "You made this with Magda Svoboda's mother, Devaty?"

"It would have been the perfect cradle for the child,"

the ancestress whispered sadly. "Had she stayed. We spent such time over the details. We were so looking forward to the adventures little Magda would have had."

"So around... 1915, maybe," Seitchman concluded. "Underhill's a little over a century old." As though it was expected, but disappointing nonetheless. "So what was there before?"

But Harry'd had enough of her leading the conversation. It didn't help that all the rest were basically clattering their cutlery on the ancient platters and miming the feast that didn't exist. It felt like the sort of tea party you might have after the Mad Hatter's funeral. "What about my great-grandfather?" he asked. "Is he around, still? Any other family?" *The Missing Element of Underhill*, he thought. *The book Granma never wrote. Because it's us. We're the royal family. We're what it's all about, and James and Jemima can piss off out of it.*

"No," the ancient woman told him. "We never keep the men. We have our servants, the Huldra, lure them, and they do their necessary work, and then they are let go. And *you* should have been a daughter. The female line is better. The male blood is subject to additional infirmities." He wasn't comfortable with her clinical gaze as she examined him. "If there were more *time*... but I shall have to do what I can with you, now you are here. I shall have to hope the analysis shows you to be sufficiently true to your heritage."

Not quite the warm welcome he'd hoped for, and he sat back, feeling like he'd failed a test set before he was born.

Seitchman had taken a phone out, to record or make notes, but had found it dead. "Let me guess," she said gloomily. "This place sucks out the power. It's at a... what, lower level of energy? That's the fairyland time difference. Like the spider said, it's an energy gradient, hard to get back up the slope. How are we even alive here?"

"Because *I* am still alive," the ancestress said proudly. "And *I* will it. And *I* am ruler of the land yet. I prioritise it to preserve human life. But I have no power or will to spare for these others, nor even for the sun to warm us. And so we have fallen, as you see. But now that the heir has returned, these things will change. A fresh influx of blood and energy into the system. A new beginning for my world, as should have happened long before."

"No more family." Harry toyed with the verdigrised fork they'd given him. Just this dried up lich of a woman, and him. The last of the Bodies. Or the Svobodas.

"But what was here before?" Seitchman asked plaintively. "Or even, what was here *first*? Carolus Svoboda, right? The old alchemist. He found his way in. So I'm guessing it wasn't all castles and forests just waiting for him. What did he find?"

"Carolus Svoboda..." The ancient lips gave the name a particular emphasis. "Carolus Magnus, greatest of all alchemists, came here and found... potential. A *genius locus* that had been waiting for the correct authority, to give shape to the void. Shape and reshape I gave it, over the generations. Until I reformed it into this place, to be the cradle to *her* daughter."

A great sad bellow from outside sent dust sifting down from the cracks in the ceiling. Harry flinched, but nobody else seemed to care.

"And then she left," Seitchman said. "After all that work." Sounding more the private investigator than the folklorist right then. Sounding as though she was about to accuse someone of murder. "So what happened?"

Before she could get an answer to that, one of the dust bunnies lurched its way up to the ancestress, clutching a filmy sheet of something that looked more like shed snakeskin than paper. Harry could see complex notation on it, reminiscent of the alchemical symbols in the book Warrington had shown him.

She smiled. Her withered skin cracked across her face in several places, with little ice-breaking sounds.

"My descendant," she breathed. "You are a fruit that has not fallen so very far from the tree. You are one of my line, despite the intervening generations. You are a suitable heir for my world."

Despite the horror of her, despite the horror of all of it, he felt a fierce surge of joy. After all, apparently he could *do* something about all the horror, once he'd settled in. "What would happen to it all if I hadn't been?" he asked.

"Then disintegration. The leaching of what energy remains until there is none. Then everything would have stopped," she said. "A heat death, it is called in the later texts. Until some other found the formulae that brought me here. If any ever did."

Harry was grinning. He couldn't help himself. *But I'm*

here. I can save it all. And then Seitchman butted in again. He was wishing he'd never brought her along.

"What happens to it all, anyway?" she wanted to know. "When you crown Harry as prince regent or whatever? All this Underhill business."

"What is that to you?" the ancestress asked archly.

"I'm a fan," Seitchman said. "I read the books, as a kid. I mean, it's not like I imagined, sure, but still. Just wondering what happens to it," and then, as Harry was about to object with, *It gets renewed, obviously*, she added, "When you've put aside childish things, you know?"

"We will have the energy for creation," the ancestress said.

"What happens to it?" Seitchman pressed, and Harry jogged her elbow to get her to shut up, but then Hulder broke in: "Tell them."

The whole batch of locals had said not a word during the 'meal,' just mummed through the motions. Now Timon and Punko and the rest were staring at the tree maid unhappily. And Harry thought about 'Huldras' being sent to lure in men, and wondered if she had a little more autonomy than the rest, as a holdover of that.

"You will be silent unless spoken to," the ancestress said, words like snapping twigs.

"Tell them," Hulder repeated. Harry sensed the attention of the room on him.

"Tell me," he echoed.

"With the energy you bring, I shall be able to salvage what remains. We will have no need of this nursery, after all," the ancestress said. "Even you must be remade, Tree-maiden. You have deteriorated past the point where you could have served your purpose. And, as he is male, we shall need a different agent to go bring a mate for him."

"Wait, what?" Harry prompted.

"A devil in the forest," the ancestress mused. "To lure a suitable maiden in."

"Okay, look, maybe we need to modernise things a little, from the way things used to work here," Harry said. "I mean, it's a connected world out there, if nothing else. The whole kidnapping aside, you really don't want to be starting that sort of conspiracy theory after whoever it is goes home. You'll be up to your eyeballs in Underlings and... Why are you all looking at me like that?"

Seitchman, the ancestress, all of the Underhill natives. Apparently he was the only one on the wrong page.

"I don't think," Seitchman said carefully, "that the previous Grooms of Underhill have wandered out of the forest with a post-coital smile on their faces. Isn't that right, Your Highness?"

"What?" Harry asked.

"I mean, there's a limited energy economy. It's like spiders, right. No offence, Smackersnack. But they eat their mates for a reason, and that's because all those eggs, that next generation, it's energy-intensive."

"I'm sure that's not the case," Harry said hurriedly. His words fell into a silence that was everyone else being sure that absolutely *was* the case.

"Your Highness," said Seitchman slowly. "You were

talking about Carolus Svoboda, the founder. How he came to this place and imposed his will on, what, a formless void? Made it his own. That must have been quite a sight. I can only imagine what he did with the place."

"It reflected the understanding of the times," the ancestress said, with a rickety shrug. "There were spheres within spheres, set out according to alchemical principles. They expressed a worldview I have since grown out of. I have read books, since. Your chemistry, your particle physics. I have composed theories, concerning what I discovered here. Not a daemon that grants wishes and must be constrained by the correct formulae, as first was thought. A machine for harnessing uncertainty, so that this small world might be whatever is wished. So long as it is fed with fresh energy. And my last leash of it is nearly up. And you, my descendant, have come at the eleventh hour, to save me."

"To save Underhill," Harry said, aware that various parts of the conversation weren't quite meshing. "We don't have to do away with it. We can repair it, keep it around. Keep them all around." Because it had dawned on him that the renewal his ancestress had been blithely talking about was a death sentence for everyone else at the table.

"I will have no need of it," the ancestress said. "And later, when there is another child to be nursemaided, it will be more efficient to create anew than to repair all this decay."

"But *I*," Harry put in, with a little more force. "I have need of it. It's Underhill. It's what I've got of my grandmother—your, what, granddaughter? It's *family*."

"Harry," said Seitchman urgently, but the ancestress actually laughed, then, spreading the cracks across her face so that a panel of her onion-layer skin peeled away, showing only more withered flesh beneath.

"This is not about *family*," she told him. "It is about the blood. You have the blood."

"So, I'm family," he insisted.

"You are a suitable vessel. The blood. The genetics, as your natural philosophers write. Sufficient compatibility."

Harry stood up, and she matched him in creaking stages.

"I'm the heir to Underhill," he insisted.

"You are the last of my line," she said. "You have come to me just in time. And you must be prepared for the transfer while I yet retain my hold in this desiccated shell."

There seemed to be a lot more dust bunnies in the hall now, and Harry abruptly decided to stop thinking of them as dust bunnies because they were really unpleasant en masse, with their broken shard eyes and their exposed fibre muscles. *Robota*, he remembered. An old Slavic word for forced labour, from an old Czech play, coined for these things by, perhaps, a very, *very* old Czech man.

"You're... Carolus," he got out. From her expression, Seitchman had worked this out a while ago. "The alchemist."

"And alchemy is mostly fable," the ancestress said—or Carolus Svoboda said, through his pirated descendant's lips. "But in this place is the secret to eternal life, so long as one can renew the vessel."

"We should have died in the cold," Hulder whispered.

"Timon, you should not have brought him." And they would have died either way, Harry understood. The only difference was that *he* was on the block now as well, and that Carolus would persist.

He did the usual thing, then: too little, too late. He leapt up and tried to make a break for it. The *robota* had him, though. Each one weak and light as sticks, but they piled on him and bore him down by sheer numbers. He heard Seitchman shout, and then cry out in pain. The whole room had erupted into chaos save for a calm space about the head of the table, from which his ancestress—his ancest*or*—watched him hauled away.

With a great shout, James held aloft the Sword of Underhill. Where a moment before, the Odlins had been advancing boldly, their ranks bristling with the barbs of their black pikes, now they quailed. The sight of the sword struck such terror into them that they ran hither and thither like ants. James led the charge of the gallant defenders of Underhill, and the Odlins were driven all the way back into the trees, out of sight of the castle. Then Wish Dog and his friends chased them all the way to the mountains at the end of the world.

The Lost Sword of Underhill (1955),
Mary Bodie, Targamane Press

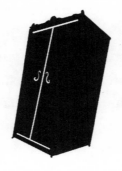

CHAPTER NINE

ANOTHER THING ABSENT from the stories was that the Castle of Underhill had dungeons. Being underground, they were actually in better nick than the chambers above, but what they'd retained in structural integrity they'd lost in amenities via the expanse of leprous, radioactive-looking fungus across one wall.

The dustling *robota* had thrown him in here, a mass of them with their naked muscles writhing and twitching to set their twig limbs in jerky motion. He had no idea what had happened to Seitchman, though likely nothing good. And indeed, *Nothing Good* felt like the motto for today's Underhill, frankly. From the overall decay to... to what he'd apparently just learned. And he'd thought *How Even Me?* would be the nadir for depressing family secrets. Honestly, he hadn't known the half of it.

He pictured himself interviewed by Margot Lorne now,

sitting in front of the museum display and cheerily saying, 'Well yes, my great-grandmother might have died in an asylum, but *her* mother was apparently just the vessel for the ghost of my more distant ancestor the mad alchemist. Who's preserved himself by, what, taking over each successive successor to the bloodline? I mean, Seitchman was asking why great-granma did a runner, and I guess that's not exactly a mystery anymore.'

He considered the timing gloomily. Apparently Carolus the arch-ancestor had been waiting for a new heir to be born before he made the switch. Did that mean he'd wait until Harry had knocked up some poor kidnapped woman before scooping out his descendant's brains like an egg and plopping his own mind into the resulting void? Was that how it worked?

You know what? I bet it isn't. I bet he's up there dusting off the alembics and sharpening the brain-spoon right now. Because, let's face it, once he'd decided to proceed with the *female* line to preserve his precious genetic code, probably the one thing Carolus hadn't been anxious to experience first-hand was childbirth. So, let the women do the hard work and then swan in and take the credit. After he and the mother-to-be had created a fantasy wonderland for the little tot to grow up in. Can't expect the great alchemist to pitch in much with the childcare, after all.

"I just wanted to be the promised prince and heir to a magical kingdom," he told the walls of his cell. "Is that so much? Is that bad of me? I mean, what did I do to earn this clusterfuck, precisely?"

"You think *you've* got problems," came a tired voice from the other side of the door.

Harry leapt up, whacking the top of his head on the low ceiling. "Timon?"

"The very same, O my great princely prince."

"Are you a prisoner too?"

"Why would they even bother?"

"Then are you... here to rescue me?"

An awkward pause. "I mean, they didn't give me the key," Timon said eventually. "And I know what you're thinking. Oh, that rascally faun, right? Lifting the key from the belt of the jailer or off a hook in the guard room. Keeping the bad guys amused with a little dance or a tune on my pipes and then sneaking down here to spring my prince. But no, not really. Didn't even think of it, to be honest. After over a century of bleak, inexorable decay, the jolly rascal kind of gets washed out of you. I'm tired, Harry."

"Well, I'm so goddamn sorry. That is obviously the saddest thing going on right now."

"Look," the faun demanded, "what do you want from me?"

"A rescue."

"Oh. Right. Well, okay, that's a reasonable request, but it's not really something I can do. I just wanted to come and... say goodbye, really. Say sorry. For whatever part I've actually played in any of this. I'm not even sure I did much, to be honest. For good or ill." A sigh that had Harry grinding his teeth. "I got your friend out, if that helps."

"Seitchman? She's okay?"

"Well, she's with Smackersnack. So she's either home and safe or in a cocoon somewhere being drained of her vital juices. You know."

"You are a useless fucker, Timon."

"I *know!*" Abruptly the ennui was gone and the faun was practically shouting through the keyhole. "I am! I was designed that way. Purposefully unable to actually achieve anything. So that your sainted grandmother could toddle through her lovely kingdom *doing* things and the rest of us could just go *Ooh* and *Aah* and applaud her. Wish Dog was to be her loyal companion and Hulder her advisor—and matchmaker, later on, but enough of that—and me? I was just the crap one who was supposed to get into trouble and get rescued and do stupid little dances and be just greedy and flawed enough to be funny. I'm the *butt* of Underhill's joke, Harry. I wish I was dead."

Harry swallowed. "I…" He wanted to throw Timon's *You think you've got problems?* back at him, but it was fairly obvious that, yes, the faun did think so, and that he was entirely correct in that regard.

"I asked Smackersnack to kill me, ages ago. Just finish me off, write me out of the story. Because *she* had run away, and abruptly I was a joke that didn't even have a punchline. But by then the bastard spider had decided she wasn't *doing* the villain thing anymore. She was already pushing her own boundaries. And so I did too. I got out. Only your world is horrible and difficult and confusing too. At least it wasn't dying. And maybe now Underhill's not dying, but that just means we all get unmade ready for what comes next. Hulder always said we should just let it go. She and Wish Dog argued all the time about what they'd do if the heir was ever found. And she was right, damn it. I should have listened to her. I should never have got involved with you."

"Timon."

There was a sniff from the other side of the door.

"I'm sorry," Harry said, sitting back down. "It doesn't help anyone, but on behalf of my whole cursed family, I'm sorry."

"Doesn't help," though Timon sounded slightly mollified. "Doesn't mean I can rescue you. Look, probably I need to go now. Get out. To your world. The big world. The Queen's started the big wheels turning, to get ready to do the thing to you. All that hoarded energy being tapped for the last time. Do you... want me to take a message to anyone?"

Harry blinked in the cell's gloom. *Tell my agent... what? Tell Toby or someone that...? Tell the Birmingham Rep I'm a bigger madman than even they were looking for?*

"You go write the world's bleakest fucking Underhill fanfic," he told the faun. "Let them know everything, even if nobody'll believe it."

"Your wish is my command, my prince." And then the hollow knocking of the faun's hooves receding. And then silence.

AND THEN SCRATCHING.

An insistent scraping noise that twitched Harry from fitful sleep. It wasn't the key in the cell door—an appropriately medieval piece of work for Carolus the alchemist. It was coming from below.

In the stories, there were things that lived below Underhill. They were always *bad* things. James and Jemima had to go fight them a couple of times to retrieve this magical McGuffin or that. They obviously hadn't tunnelled up under the actual castle at any point. Except that was in the books, and that was when Underhill was Working As Intended. What worms gnawed the kingdom's bones right now, he couldn't imagine.

Or, actually, he *could* imagine. All too well.

After a moment's indecision, he decided being eaten alive by worm monsters was worse than being sacrificed by your alchemist forebear, and began rattling the door and shouting. Every so often he stopped and the chewing, gnawing sound was definitely closer, definitely right underfoot. He could feel the shudder and thrum as the *thing* approached him. His yells died to a little whimper, because when he shouted, he couldn't hear it, and if he couldn't hear it, then he wouldn't know when it was about to break through. And for some reason he really *had* to know that fatal moment, even though the knowledge wouldn't exactly bring him any joy.

"Help," he croaked, at last, and then the floor collapsed in a shower of mouldy stone and fungus and he was carried with it into darkness.

And light. The bright, actinic beam of a very modern torch. For a moment it was all he could see and then, after some squabbling, it was shifted from his eyes to illuminate…

faces. A lot of quite nasty faces. They had slit noses and big ears and squinty wrinkled creases where their eyes should be. They were hairy, and they were patently falling apart just like everything else. Some wore corroded armour of overlapping plates, and some had eyebrows that twisted forwards into long antennae. There was something of the burrowing insect to all of them.

Odlins, he thought. An occasional menace who turned up whenever Underhill needed a dose of mild threat, and were then soundly beaten and sent back to the mountains. And now, apparently, they were getting their revenge by stealing the heir to the throne, and that seemed on-message for them and Harry couldn't blame them for it.

They pushed and shoved him through a succession of tunnels and caves, sometimes with the torch on, sometimes off, sometimes winding it furiously to get the beam going again. And he realised they hadn't just dug all the way. The whole of the earth beneath the castle was swiss-cheesed with holes, and here and there caustic fungus was eating away at everything. He was amazed the edifice above hadn't just collapsed into the depths. Perhaps that would be Underhill's final knell, before the last dregs of energy left and everything stopped forever.

And then out. What he thought was just a larger cavern became the barren sky above as they emerged from a cave mouth lit by the corpselight of luminous mushrooms.

And Seitchman.

He stopped, staring at her. She'd gone native. Lawyer, PI, academic and now, apparently, fantasy hero. Someone had found her a coat of mail that had probably been shiny once but was now mostly rust and string. She had a tattered cloak and there was an actual honest-to-God sword in her hand.

Hulder was with her on one side, and Timon skulking on the other. The faun gave Harry a sheepish look as if to say, *This isn't my doing. Just comic relief, remember?*

The Odlins lurched and skittered and slouched until they'd formed almost an honour guard around her. Any moment and they'd be warming their hands against her like she was a fire. Seitchman herself looked mostly embarrassed by it.

"That was quick work, though," she said. "In and out in sixty seconds, almost."

"We have been planning for a long time," Hulder told her.

"Planning what?" Harry demanded of them. He sat down, where the shadow of the cave mouth meant there was less of the non-snow to sink into. The ground felt spongy beneath him, the rock soft enough to dig his nails in.

Seitchman obviously expected some sort of revolutionary manifesto too. Hulder just shrugged, shoulders hunching inwards until Harry could see the broken edges, the concavity of her.

"Just... planning. A means without an end. In case an end came along. But what could any of us do? You cannot depose the god who made you. We were always dying, from the start. If the mother had never fled, we'd have served our purpose and been put out of our misery long ago. We only hung on this long because she left. And if you had never come here, we'd die out in the end, when our creator died and the final cold came. Back to the dust we were raised from." She didn't sound bitter, just philosophical. "And if our creator made your body a new house for their mind, then the land would live, but we would die. There would be enough energy to unmake us and create something new. Wish Dog preferred that latter death. I choose the former. Let there be an end to everything."

"You were sent to bring men into this world," Harry recalled.

"Or those like me. Before he remade me as a nursemaid. And there may be those like me again. But not me. I'm broken. And I'm sick of it. We were none of us meant to last this long."

They trekked a while through the forest. Distantly there was a long howl—the dog, not the clown. Presumably Harry was still a beacon to everything in the world. It wasn't as though he could just put a cloak on and pretend to be an Odlin. Eventually he began to see the mist-like drifts of web half-invisible between the trees and knew where they had come. Back where he'd fled before. Smackersnack's lair.

The spider crept out from the dark when they stopped, round eyes fixed on Harry. Timon broke shards off the nearest trees and started a sickly-looking fire.

"Biscuit?" Seitchman asked him. And of course he was ravenous at the thought. The grand homecoming feast at the castle had been something of a bust, on the calorific side of things. She had a packet of bourbons, and he scarfed a couple down gratefully.

"You're the Odlin king now, are you?"

"I don't think I've got the codpiece to pull that off," she said. "Hulder led me to them. And they're up for anything, these boys."

He glanced from the Odlins to the spider. "We seem to be the bad guys," he pointed out.

"Why?"

"Well... because these are the bad guys. Threats to Underhill."

"Firstly, Underhill is the creation and personal property of a body-stealing wizard who's effectively murdered multiple generations of his own descendants," Seitchman pointed out. "Secondly, they're not. I mean, I guess they were meant to be, but none of that actually *happened*. All that book stuff, based on your great-grandma's stories, it's... how it was *supposed* to go, I guess. How it was set up to play out. Except no kid, no adventures. No actual villainies perpetrated." She had sat down by the fire and the Odlins clustered close. They looked... almost healthy. Slightly less dying. Seitchman saw his look and nodded.

"It's us," she told him. "I thought so earlier, when it was just me. Now there's two of us... We're high energy creatures, you and me. We're feeding them, just by being near them. Look, I've been thinking about what this place is."

"Aside from 'magic kingdom'?"

"I don't know that I believe in magic," she confessed.

"You went looking for Underhill without believing in magic?"

"Weirdest thing. I *did* believe. Right up until I got here, and especially until we got chatting to old Carolus. Only...

He was talking about *Einstein*. And the old alchemists wouldn't have called themselves magicians. They were scientists, as much as anyone was. And… Okay, so listen to me. A little psycho-reactive bubble world, okay? Forget the magic or the not of it, that's what we've got here."

"If you say so."

"Your man Carolus studied all the occult learning he could get, and he was likely the prime folklorist of his day, too. He collected stories about people going into fairyland. I've read some of his work. He compiled lists of things to do or not to—times, places, rituals. And there's a crapton of this stuff, basically. Traditions all across Europe. Kingdoms under hills, in lakes, in the heart of the wood. Places that are vast and yet touch the human world only at certain points. Lots of commonalities that my more level-headed colleagues would say is just the same story getting twisted in the telling as it moves from place to place. But which I always fondly imagined might be because there was a *truth* at the heart of it. Because I was, to be frank, a very bad folklorist. But here we are: a place your ancestor found and made his own, to his desire. Where he can, at the height of his power, literally reshape the entire little bubble-world and create actual *people*, independent sentient entities, to serve his whims. And he can send Hulder back to our world on her hunk-fishing expeditions. And some of the denizens can even get out under their *own* steam. There is, basically, a navigable path, a decipherable method to get in and out."

"I haven't heard anything yet that doesn't just scream 'magic,'" Harry admitted.

"I think we're looking at one of two things," Seitchman said. "We're looking at a natural property of reality, that these bubbles form and then, for some damn reason, just do what you want if you're a thinking being who can work out how to get into them. Or they're not natural."

"Magic."

"I mean, I was thinking aliens, to be honest."

"Fucking what now?" He felt weirdly offended that someone was bringing *aliens* into his nice magic.

"Seems to me to make more sense that something *built* this space with all the psychic mod cons, than you're relying on the, what, the quantum uncertainty principle or some damn thing to just give you the goods. Seems more likely there's some supercomputer woven into the structure of this that's all 'What is your wish, O master?' than that the universe is just that useful on its own."

Harry shrugged. "I don't think we're really in a position to talk about 'likely,' are we? Maybe Carolus knows enough to start placing bets, but us? Not so much."

"Speaking of…" And Hulder stuttered, and would not actually say the alchemist's name. "He is coming."

"Yeah?" Seitchman stood, shrugging the rusted mail more evenly across her shoulders.

"Wait, what?" Harry demanded.

"He has begun his ritual," Hulder said. "He has committed his reserves of power and half-loosed his mind from its old home. Now he must have you, and soon, or it is all wasted, and probably he cannot do it again. There is a clock, now, that there was not before. And we will be waiting."

"I'm *bait?*" Harry demanded.

"Only for a little longer," Seitchman said.

"What is going on?"

"What's going on is, you have to make a choice about what you want to do," she told him. "I guess I do too. Because Hulder and the Odlins' new plan is to have a great big throwdown fight and maybe kill their creator. Because if they're going to die, they may as well bring the whole thing to an end. When he was holed up in the castle, that was never an option, but now they've got the one thing he wants."

"And me?"

Smackersnack stepped forwards. "Elementary to engineer an escape," she remarked. "I also abscond. Timon too."

The faun shrugged miserably.

"You can get the hell out, basically. When Carolus pitches up, you've done your job," Seitchman confirmed. "I probably should, too."

Harry looked at her armour and the sword. "You're not going to, though, are you?"

"Maybe after we've killed the bastard."

Make a choice, she said. And he'd only been offered one option, which perhaps showed the general level of regard the creatures of Underhill had for their promised prince.

I could go, and you can come get me after you win... he thought cravenly, but of course that would probably bring him out in the real world around, what, June, July? Long after the whole pandemic thing was over, surely. Back to work, filming restarted and theatres open and perhaps the

job at the Birmingham Rep would still be going, and...
and by then Underhill would be cold and dead, just stilled
remains buried beneath the drifting non-snow. Just a
memory he'd soon convince himself was a hallucination.

"What if I stay?" he asked.

When James and Jemima stepped past the last trees, of course they saw nothing but the familiar meadow stretching out before them. Beyond it, as though they had never left, was their grandmother's house. Grandmother herself was just stepping out of the little white-painted back door, shading her eyes with her hand, ready to call them in for lunch. For they knew that, no matter how often they visited Underhill, and no matter what adventures they should have, they would always find themselves home and safe in the end.

The Horns of Underhill (1954),
Mary Bodie, Targamane Press

CHAPTER TEN

It was, of course, the sixty-four-thousand-dollar question, or whatever collapsing currency might even apply to Underhill. And the answer was that nobody really knew. What if Harry, promised prince, actually pulled his finger out and stuck around to fight the wicked usurper? And while, politically, Carolus Svoboda was the diametrical opposite of a usurper, Harry reckoned the label still applied to someone who had his mind transplanted into the bodies of his descendants to achieve eternal life.

"What did he even do with it?" he wanted to know. "Stuck here in his bubble?"

"Well, unless Einstein somehow paid him a visit, I'd guess he's kept tabs on the real world," Seitchman pointed out. "He has seductive tree women out there to go bring in sperm donors. I guess he probably sends out book-spiders or library-fauns to help him keep on top of the scientific literature." She had her sword out and was making awkward passes with it.

"Do you know how to use that thing?" Harry asked her.

"Not a fucking clue, no," she admitted.

"You weren't captain of the fencing team at Whateverthehell College, Oxford?"

"I was not, no."

"Why are you even still here?"

She stopped flailing around and looked at him, opened her mouth to answer, shrugged.

"I mean, I appreciate the rescue, but Smackersnack could just poop you out to the real world now. You could go write a thesis or something."

"So could you. Or a comedy skit, anyway."

"Except this is actually my fight. By right of bloodline. I am, insofar as anyone is, responsible for all the goddamn misery in this world." And that was mendacious, of course. It wasn't actually culpability that was keeping him here. It was that, in the falling ruins of Underhill, he was, for one brief moment, important. A vile, self-serving business, but apparently it could look like noble sacrifice if you squinted really hard at it.

Seitchman carefully fed the sword into her belt. "I," she said, "really liked the *Underhill* books. They were why I started studying folklore. They were the thing that kept me sane as a kid when my folks broke up. And there was always something, you know? When I started to look behind the actual texts, when I found out about the Underlings. There were always people treating them way more seriously than you'd think. And now, look here, it's real—even if it wasn't ever really real. I mean, when Carolus and your great-grandma made it, it wasn't real. It was a fake fantasy world to amuse the kid who was on the way, so Carolus could eat her mum and keep on living forever. But it's *become* real. Not just like the books, but it's been sitting around for a hundred years now. All those characters have been living their lives in it. And... I want to help them. I feel I know them, they're old friends, even if they're not *really* the characters I read about."

Then Hulder was striding past them in all her shattered eggshell glory. "They're coming!" Her voice raised high, startling the Odlins from their holes and shadows. "They're here! Rouse yourselves."

"Must be a scary moment when your actual creator turns up to give you a smack," Seitchman said.

There was maybe a score of Odlins all told, a ragged band of hunched, hairy creatures clutching knives and crooked spears and sharpened pieces of not-wood, plus one who had a very modern-looking pipe wrench polished to a silver shine. They wore hides and rags and tarpaulins, and one had a baseball cap and another a bright yellow anorak. There had, Harry gathered, been foraging expeditions into the real. Added to the Odlins they had Smackersnack, Hulder and the reluctant Timon, a pair of spiky-backed lizards, an animated statue missing one arm and a chicken-headed bear whose precise function in the books Harry couldn't remember.

And, coming through the trees, he could see the might of his ancestor's forces, silhouetted against the leprous glare of the non-snow.

There were some of the wiry dustling *robota*, loping along now on two legs, now on four. Not as many as he'd seen in the castle, so either the rest had vital housework to be getting on with or they didn't do well in the outdoors. There was Wish Dog, of course; a slavering hound the size of a horse with enough intact skin for half a horse was a fearsome thing. There was one dissident Odlin and a couple of armed fauns, a winged man with a spear, and a pair of extremely moth-eaten lions. And that was it.

They'd never made a big budget film of the Underhill books, but Harry had seen the one they'd done of the *other* series, and the big set piece battle at the end had impressed him mightily. And there had been the Tolkien films, too, and they'd also leant rather magnificently into great big fights. That was, his cultural touchstones insisted, how these things ended.

The assembled might of Underhill, on both sides, looked rather as if an extremely under-funded re-enactment society had decided to pay tribute to that kind of Grand Clash of Powers, and almost nobody had turned up.

Harry was willing to bet that the awkward, foot-shuffling pause that developed after the loyalists arrived would also not have featured in a big budget Hollywood adaptation, though it was probably something that actual history had seen quite a bit.

Eventually, Wish Dog padded forwards. In the books, he'd had a pack of other lovely perfect dogs to romp around and be a deus ex machina with. Harry wondered what had happened to them. From the look of the furs, some of them were being worn by the Odlins.

"What," the dog growled, "is your game plan here, exactly? And if you do anything with that stick, Timon, I will chew your fucking arm off."

"Where's Carolus?" Seitchman demanded.

"Takes our lord and master a while to get going these days. On account of he's *dying* and needs us to *save* him so that everything doesn't just *end*." A raw eye rolled until it was pointing at the tree maid. "The *world*, Hulder. The actual end of the world. Which we can prevent. If you just hand over that human man there."

"Our world ends either way," Hulder said simply. "It just means we get swept aside for something else."

"But *something* goes on," Wish Dog pointed out.

"No," Seitchman broke in. "Some*one* goes on. The same someone. A four-hundred-year-old alchemist kin-vampire. Someone who wants to live that much, and will kill every one of you in the blink of an eye the moment they have the power to do so."

"He made us," Wish Dog said, but Timon broke in.

"Oh, not the loyal dog thing again. You're not even a dog. Have you looked in the mirror lately? Get one of those creepy muppets over and look into their eyes. You're not a dog. You don't have to do the *His Master's Voice* thing."

"But it's *everything dies*, or *almost everything dies*," Wish Dog set out for him, as for a child.

"Not necessarily." It was the first word Harry had been able to get in edgeways. Somehow even Seitchman seemed to be more a part of what was going on. He had been entirely relegated to 'trophy.' "What if I could change things?"

Wish Dog's exposed musculature writhed over honeycombed bone. It was not clear, between the decay and the general dogginess, what expression he was trying for, but Harry reckoned it was sneering.

"You're nothing," the dog told him. "The vessel, that's what *he* calls you."

"I'm the *heir*." Knowing it was the purest nonsense. Storybook logic. But then, even though they were none of them the actual storybook characters, they'd been made in that vein. He saw Wish Dog flinch at the word.

And then something was coming through the trees, something big. The delay in Carolus's arrival had not just been creaking old joints and the need to wrap up warm before leaving the house. He'd been sorting out an appropriate conveyance.

It broke the trees on its way to them—not the splintering of wood, but hollow cracks and pops as the brittle fibreglassy substance of the trunks gave way. You couldn't say the thing *strode*, because of course Gombles had never really had legs, exactly. Just feet and a great sack of a body, now bloated out further by some internal process of decay and dissolution. The clown's boneless arms flailed, four-digited hands barely visible in the darkness overhead. Its eyes, each wider than Harry was tall, stared and rolled independently. But apparently Carolus hadn't been willing to put up with the wretched creature's wailing, because he'd had his minions sew its mouth shut.

They'd built a kind of howdah around the clown's... well, not shoulders, as the thing didn't have them, but where the shoulders would otherwise have been. On one side stood a couple of the dustlings, armed with spears. On the other, swathed in blankets and propped up in a padded chair, was Carolus Svoboda, or at least the withered body that was his current vessel.

One last tree broke under the clown's body before silence descended. The boldness of Hulder's little force seemed to have drained out through their boots, now their actual creator had arrived. For his part, the ancient alchemist just huddled back in his seat and glowered myopically down at them, as though he'd forgotten why he'd come out.

At last, though, the quavering old woman's voice piped down peevishly, "Well? You haven't killed or exiled the vessel. I presume, therefore, that you have some demand or other?"

Harry looked to Hulder, to find her looking at him. He tried Timon; the same. In fact, quite a lot of people seemed to think he had an answer. Only Seitchman knew him well enough to discount any such thing, standing forwards and tilting her head back to call up.

"What do *you* want?" she demanded. "How many generations of your own family have you devoured, just to keep living? And why? What's all that waste for?"

"Ah, that." Carolus hunched forwards, gripping the rails. "Would it help to ask who you even *are*, that you've decided to interfere with my business? You were some sort of scholar?"

"Concerned bystander," Seitchman replied. She had her sword in her hand, though Harry didn't feel it would do much to help her if Gombles got going again.

"Thanks to the gifts of this world I've inhabited fourteen separate vessels since leaving my original body. All of my family, as you say, because genetic variance makes the transfer of consciousness more difficult. You make it sound as though it were somehow *worse* than taking the bodies of random strangers; a curious morality. And as to *why*... You are a scholar, hence you must understand there is a platonic goal for all learning, of which all other purposes are merely shadows. The perfection of matter, from the base to the precious, from that which decays to that which is eternal."

"And this is precious and perfect to you, is it?" Seitchman demanded.

"It is a work in progress," Carolus said imperturbably. "But the tools I am provided with here permit me to continue my studies, aided by the greatest writings of the world I left behind. I have found an approximation of the eternal life we all sought, back at Rudolph's court. A means to turn this hoary age into youth again. When I re-energise this space once more, I can even manufacture gold out of dust and nothing, though gold was only ever a side-effect of our great quest for perfection."

"Eternal life on a mound of corpses."

"A thousand blades of grass must die for each beast of the field to live. Cattle and deer and the fish of the sea must die, that wolves and men may live. All life is a pyramid of corpses," Carolus pronounced. "My researches have established that there are two basic principles behind attaining eternal life. Firstly, that it is achieved over the corpses of others; secondly, that just as the nature of perfection is singular, so is the eternal life bestowed. I have made myself the apex of the pyramid. In prolonging myself thus, I am merely becoming an expression of the basic nature of the universe."

"How convenient for you. And these, your creations, you'll just snuff them out too, once you've the power to do so? Living things, thinking things."

"You are like a man who talks to his dog and thinks the hound understands every word," Carolus scoffed, making Wish Dog cock his single ear and whine uncertainly. "They appear real to you, because you didn't bring them into being. They comprise merely sophisticated *roboty* that have grown eccentric and unruly from being left to work for too long."

"*Roboty*, as in forced workers. Paying rent in labour just for the privilege of existing."

Carolus shrugged. "Without me they wouldn't exist. They serve me as angels serve divinity, should such a divinity even exist. I have, over the years, ceased to be convinced of the proposition, but perhaps after another century or so of study I shall reconsider. Now, you have my vessel. What do you and your rebellious angels demand? They want to escape this place and go into the wider world? I know they have that within their grasp, and I permit it. They want some riches or goods or benison, once I am returned to my youth and strength? Then let us have your demands. All things shall be within my power once the land and I are re-energised. You can all go and live as princes, if that's to your taste. Why should I care?"

"All the kingdoms of the Earth, is it?" Seitchman asked.

"Tiresomely quoting scripture, out of context and for mere effect, was ever a tedious quality of scholars," Carolus told her. "Just let me have your demands and then give me my vessel."

"Er," Harry said, because apparently he was a hostage now.

"I think that's covered the negotiation stage of things," Seitchman decided. "Do we fight now, or what?"

And, for a moment, literally nobody knew. Everyone on both sides just stood there while Carolus tutted and plucked at his shawl. The *Underhill* books had been full of adventures and skirmishes, but none of those things had ever happened, here. The land had grown senile waiting for them, and forgotten what it was for.

Then Timon stepped forwards. "You missed the part where you talk about *responsibility*," he called up, and Harry saw the faun was shaking with emotion. "You made us, you and her. You made us for a purpose we never got to fulfil. I was meant to be *funny*. I was meant to have *adventures*. To get into scrapes and be rescued and never learn my lesson so it happened again and again. I'm Timon the rascally faun! Except I never got to be. And now *look at me!* Any child would run screaming, now. I'm ruined, and I never got to be *me!* And it's been more than a human lifetime, living like this, and you did nothing."

"Are you suggesting I should just have kidnapped some random human child to keep you amused?" Carolus mocked.

"Fucking *yes!*" Timon said, and in that moment of flipped morality he took one long step forwards and cast the spear he was holding.

It was a good throw, and his long-boned frame was made for it. He didn't get Carolus, but he got Gombles right in the vast expanse of the clown's right eye. And after that, there wasn't really any option but to have the big fight, for what it was worth.

It was not the glorious big budget clash of armies. Everyone just scattered and then attacked whoever didn't seem to be paying them attention, and then only half-heartedly. The dustlings went at it with a will, but they were jerky and uncoordinated, the last bargain-bin products of the Underhill creation process after the world had gone far beyond its sell-by date. And everyone else there... well, they knew each other, of course. They were, if not exactly old friends, then at least acquaintances of a respectable vintage. So Wish Dog romped through the fray like a freight train, but he didn't actually hit anyone head on, nor savage them with his jaws, just knocked people over. And Smackersnack leapt on a faun and tied the thing to a tree, but her fangs remained discreetly sheathed. Everyone danced about each other and shouted insults and waved sticks, no closer to actually inflicting serious harm than rowdy schoolchildren.

Seitchman tried to wade in with her sword, and perhaps she had neither their reservations nor their protections, but nobody much wanted to go near her. The enemy were shy of her and her allies didn't know what to do with her. And as for Harry...

He decided he needed to act. Otherwise he was consenting to just being the trophy rather than a participant. He grabbed up a heavy stick someone had dropped and tried to find someone to fight, but everyone was terrified of hurting him. And then Wish Dog just bounded up like a happy puppy and grabbed him by the collar, lifting him half off the ground.

"Right," the mutt mumbled, and started to drag him towards the sagging mountain of flesh that was the clown. Then Smackersnack dropped onto Wish Dog's back and the pair of them broke apart, bared teeth and fangs and a lot of threat, and Harry between them.

He whacked Wish Dog across the muzzle with his stick and the dog yelped so wretchedly he instantly felt bad about it. He locked gazes, eye to flayed eye.

He raised the stick again.

"Don't—" Wish Dog started, and then Harry threw his weapon off between the trees and, with a hiss of annoyance, the hound rushed off to retrieve it.

"Go do something about Gombles," he told the spider, with a sudden inspiration. "Wrap your webs around its legs so it falls over."

"Lacks legs," Smackersnack pointed out, and then Gombles decided the matter by looming over them and snatching Harry up in one balloon-fingered hand.

He waited for the crushing pressure, but of course Carolus needed him intact. Instead, utterly uninterested in the rest of the scrum below, the alchemist just hauled on the reins and had Gombles turn awkwardly around, ready to return to the castle. Those traces, Harry saw, were fixed into the rims of the clown's vast, ever-open eyes. A yellowish fluid oozed from the wounds where the hooks went in, as well as from Timon's spear, which still quivered at the edge of Gombles' right pupil. A strangled weeping sound crawled constantly from between the stitches that held its mouth closed. And while Harry, man and child, had always loathed the clown, no monster deserved that.

He howled at the thing to let him go, promised it he'd free it from the hooks, but Gombles was a slave to its pain and just shook him, its rubbery arm rippling like a serpent. Then Smackersnack was there, scaling the sagging foothills of Mount Gombles and trying to attack the howdah. The dustlings jabbed at her with their spears, and Harry saw one of her legs just crumple and fall off. She leapt at them, and a moment later her weight had carried off that side of the howdah entirely, leaving the upper slopes to Carolus, whose world was now slipping dangerously sideways.

The alchemist's withered lips were bared in a snarl of determination. His eyes—Harry's great-great-grandmother's stolen eyes—were as wide as Gombles' own as he clung to the rail and yanked on the reins, then began beating at the side of the clown's head with a barbed goad. Harry was swooped dizzyingly through the air, over the jagged broken teeth of the trees. "Will you stop!" he yelled. "Will you just stop!"

"Never!" Carolus spat at him, meaning not the current fray, but existence as a whole. Never let go. Never give up. Never die, no matter what. A man who'd made his own purgatory four centuries back and intended to suffer there forever because extinction was worse.

The fighting at its back now, Gombles took a lurching step towards the castle. And halted.

A lone figure stood there, silhouetted against the snow. A ravaged hound the size of a pony. Carefully, it put down the stick.

"Make sure nothing follows us," Carolus shouted, but his voice was thin and reedy, and Harry drew in all the breath he could manage and hollered out, "Fetch, boy! Fetch the spear! Fetch!"

There was a moment of connection between him and the dog, in which Wish Dog wanted him to know exactly how disgusted he was with the whole business. The sheer *dogginess* imposed on him; the unbearable burden of living up to being the Best Dog in the World. A moment in which Wish Dog wanted Harry to know that he absolutely had a *choice* over how to interpret the command, and that Harry's voice was a world away from His Master's.

On which basis, and for no master but himself, Wish Dog bunched his rotting hindquarters and vaulted up Gombles' sagging sides, clawing his way upwards, swift as the wind. *Wish Dog! Wish Dog! The old deus ex machina grinding its gears into motion one last time!* Vaulting from the trampoline of Gombles' paunch, springing so high that Harry saw sinews part in the decaying hound's legs. Jaws closing about the shaft of the spear and ripping it free as gravity caught up with events and yanked him back down.

A shrill squeal erupted from somewhere within Gombles

and it slapped at its face with both hands. The howdah lurched another twenty degrees from the horizontal and Harry was abruptly not *in* the hand but clinging to it, showered in piss-coloured ichor as Gombles clutched at the ragged wound.

He ended up at the howdah, at its rail, hanging from it, staring up into the time-eroded face of his ancestor.

Carolus reached out and snagged him. For a moment a heartfelt family reconciliation was on the cards. Then Wish Dog was there again, and this time he'd brought a friend. Seitchman was *riding* him, or at least holding on to the remaining handfuls of mouldy fur.

She lashed out with her sword, and Carolus shrieked and quailed back. The blade ended up gashing Gombles' face and severing the stitches at one corner of its broad mouth. The taut thread instantly unravelled, dragging through the needle holes as the vast orifice gaped open in a howl.

Then Seitchman had Harry, and the three of them were descending, James and Jemima on Wish Dog's back, bouncing painfully off Gombles' flank before crashing down at the feet of Hulder and Timon and Smackersnack.

Above them, Gombles reeled, and its pitiful voice roared out in agony. Carolus cast about for the reins, but the alchemist had dropped them as he flinched away from the sword. The clown was on its own terrible recognizance.

For a moment it just loomed there, taller than trees, vaster than anything in the world of Underhill except the castle itself. A scaling error, a mistake, and a profoundly bad idea even in its original conception. The happy, bouncy clown nobody had really ever found funny. Except Granma Magda, for some reason, and for her sake Harry could find pity in his heart for Gombles. And inspiration.

"Gombles!" he shouted at the top of his voice. "Whatever you do, don't eat the queen!"

Carolus, as the howdah sagged still further, lashed at the clown with his goad, shrieking orders, but something obviously got through to whatever served the monster as a mind. One of its hideous rubbery hands plucked the alchemist from his roost and held him aloft.

"Eat the queen?" the monstrous clown boomed, a hideous echo of the books' one and only running joke. "I shall!" and Gombles dumped Carolus into that newly freed maw.

"We will always come back when
Underhill is threatened,"
Jemima assured them.
"Underhill will always find
us. There will be a door, or
a path into the woods, or a _really_
flicking
rabbit hole, ~~or a wardrobe~~ _the noses_
of their
that will lead us here." _lawyers_
now,
Magda!

James nodded solemnly and
held out the Sword, hilt-
first, and Wish Dog took the
weapon in his jaws. "You must
hold this for us. We'll need
it when we come next."

Then they turned and began
Aren't
they walking along the trail
with
their they knew would lead back to
aunt
this ~~Granma's~~ turning to wave to...
time?

The Last of Underhill: Fragments and
incomplete writings of Mary Bodie [1969],
Thomas Naiston, Patroclus Press

CHAPTER ELEVEN

It was getting colder.

They'd retreated to the castle, and Harry had fondly hoped that a diligent search might reveal a control room, preferably with a big switch. *Have you tried turning your magical kingdom off and on again?*

No, just off.

There was nothing but ruin, though. Decaying rooms with ceilings shot full of holes, only the lightless void beyond; arcades of tumbled arches; the thousand varieties of fungus; stones soft as overripe fruit to the touch, bulging like pustules beneath the weight of those above. And the cold, creeping in, riming it all with frost. Turning the gills of the mushrooms into delicate traceries of white. The non-snow sifting endlessly down as though the dark vault above was disintegrating.

He and Seitchman roamed the castle, and everyone else followed. He kept trying to get away from them, from Timon and Hulder, Wish Dog and the rest. Because of their eyes. Because of their beseeching gazes. The promised prince, come to save the kingdom. Except he didn't know how, and very obviously Carolus's death had just accelerated whatever demise had already been underway.

The dustlings, those stick-and-string budget minions, had all just collapsed into bits. If there was some secret part of the castle, then nobody could find it. And yet they all just clustered close to him and stared with a terrible hope. As though he could reach into a hat with a magicianly flourish and produce a better future. Or *any* future.

"I should have let him take me," Harry decided eventually.

"They'd all still be dead," Seitchman pointed out reasonably. "Look, I've been talking to the spider, about options."

"She can get them all out," Harry agreed. "To the real world. For what that's worth. I mean, it's not much and they won't exactly blend in, but it's not... *this*."

"Timon's held down a few jobs, cash in hand, he said," Seitchman observed. "Cleaning, factory line, checkout clerk. Even worked in a kebab place for a month. Says they asked him if he was authentically Greek. I mean, he's a faun. I guess that counts?"

Harry shook his head. "You're going to help them get set up over there?"

"I don't have much in the way of resources—can't exactly set up the Rebecca Seitchman Home For Displaced Fictional Characters—but I'll do what I can."

Harry nodded. "You think this happens a lot?"

"What?"

"You think other books might be... I mean, for all we know, Aslan's in a zoo enclosure at Longleat and Frodo works the night shift at an Amazon warehouse."

Seitchman stared at him. "That," she said, "is a weird fucking thought." But she sounded oddly intrigued.

He'd assumed they'd leave him alone if he left the castle, but every damn denizen of the place followed him out into the woods. It was really bad there, the trees riven with ice, more than half of them just jagged stumps. The drifts of white cosmic dandruff become pincushions of broken shards. And it was all hollow, all just set dressing now he could see the insides of everything. Carolus hadn't really known or cared how trees worked. Or people, judging by the emptiness of Hulder. Would they even last, in the real world? Or would the hard physics of Einstein and Newton grind them down without their native environment to provide them with energy and motion?

After a while in the woods the ice had begun to melt, and he had a moment's dreadful triumph that *Yes, I am bringing the spring back again!* as though he really was a mythic king and any moment the sun would rise. And then he realised he was both right, in a profoundly small way, and wrong. He wasn't bringing life back to the world. He was warming it. He was a source of power, a creature from a higher energy place slumming it here in Underhill. Timon and the others followed him and Seitchman because the place was just plain *warmer* wherever they went. But it wasn't life. He was just slowly bleeding his energy out into the void.

I haven't even felt hungry since I got here. Some fundamental elements of energy conservation worked differently in the world Carolus had set up. The alchemist hadn't wanted to be bothered with packing lunches for eternity. The elaborate children's toys created for a baby never born here weren't intended to be a functioning ecosystem; just a complex clockwork that would eventually wind down.

Around the time he was having *that* revelation, he managed to trip into a drift that was deeper than expected, ramming his knee into a piece of broken tree really quite painfully. And the denizens looked at him and were slow to actually help him up. Because, he knew, it didn't really matter to them whether he was here or there, standing up or lying down. He was patently no use to them other than as a meagre flame to warm themselves by, for a little while. Until the last bit of life seeped out of their world, and the only option would be to flee it for Harry's own.

Back in the castle, limping along with the aid of a stick Hulder had found for him, he gathered them all together.

"I'm sorry," he said. There were maybe thirty denizens there by then. Every creature of Underhill that could reach the castle, and the huge bulk of Gombles, even, leaning in over the crumbled edge of one wall. "My family has royally screwed you all over. Made you for a purpose that didn't happen. Abandoned you. Never cared about you. I'm so sorry. I have tried to... what? *Connect* with this place. Bring it back, breathe life into it. But I'm not a medieval alchemist. I have no idea what Carolus did, that first time."

Looking from face to face for... what? Forgiveness? All he found was hunger and the terrible knife of hope. Save for Smackersnack, whose plate-eyed attention was on Seitchman as the two of them conspired at the back.

Timon had one hand on Wish Dog's head. The hound's tormented gaze was the hardest to meet, Harry found. There was just enough genuine doggy faith in it, no matter what skin and flesh had peeled away.

"I think we always knew that we were doomed," the faun said. Not exactly letting Harry off the hook, but perhaps sugaring the pill a little. "It's hard, though, to know your creator didn't even care enough to put you out of your misery. To be so thoroughly abandoned by your maker."

Harry stared at him for a long time, and then said, "Not both of them."

Timon exchanged a blank look with Hulder. "You what now?"

"My great-grandmother. The one who fled. She fled because she worked out what Carolus would do to her once the child was born, I assume, but… she was there when you were made. She must have had an input, even if Carolus did the actual making to her order. And she had a rough time, in my world. They locked her up. They thought she was mad. But they let her see her daughter, and when they were together, she told stories. Stories of you, of here. And her daughter, when she was older, wrote them down, and they got made into books that thousands of people read, and there was a cartoon and pyjamas and a lunch box and a frankly rather terrifying East European stop-motion adaptation and… But my point is, *she* did care. Devaty, my great-grandmother, your co-creator. She really did. She wanted you to live, for her daughter. I appreciate it's not much of a consolation, but she made you all her kid's playmates, her childhood friends. In the only way she could. Whenever they let the girl visit her."

"Yeah, I don't know how much that actually helps," said Timon tiredly, but one of the Odlins piped up, "Tell us."

"What?" Harry asked, wrongfooted.

"Yes, tell us," Hulder agreed. "Tell us about Underhill."

"But you… know," Harry started. Except of course they didn't. They were the blank starting state for the books, but the actual *events* had never happened here. The engine of Underhill had been all wound up for a bold child to have adventures with the whimsical forest folk. And then the spring had just slowly lost tension over a century of disuse.

And so he told them, as best he could remember. The Cliff Notes version of most of the Underhill books, getting it wrong here and there and smudging one volume into another, but overall giving a creditable account of his grandmother's work. Told them about the adventures they might have had, had things gone differently. The battles they'd have fought, the villainies, their own deaths in some cases, both comic and tragic. The somewhat saccharine heroism of James and Jemima, who were even more fictional than they.

Around about the fourth book—or possibly the fifth, because they were a bit samey and he was getting confused over details—he realised he was crying. For his great-grandmother who had died in an institution, and for his grandmother whom he'd never met. For Underhill, which had been so meticulously crafted and yet been still-born from the start. For generations of his family, devoured by

Carolus, and for Carolus—for surely the old man must have had *some* virtue to him, to set all this madness in motion. And for himself, his petty ambitions and rivalries and bad choices. He had to keep stopping and wiping his nose on his sleeve, drying his eyes and then soldiering on. A litany of faintly twee escapades and rescues, object quests and slap-up feasts back at the castle. Always home in time for tea, and Underhill waiting when the next book rolled around.

By the time he had finished, the silence in the ruined hall was so intense that he thought he'd talked them to death. That the world around them had just flatlined during his raconteuring, and that was that. They were genuinely rapt, though. Felix 'Harry' Bodie had actually given the performance of a lifetime, and he hadn't even realised he was doing it.

"That was the last one," he whispered into that chasming quiet. "Sorry. I think she meant to do more but... well, it was cancer. It was quick, Mum said."

Silence.

"That's all I've got."

Silence.

"You can stop staring at me now."

"Your stick," said Hulder.

He didn't understand, assumed he'd misheard. *I'm stuck? I mean, yes, I guess I am.* But she stepped forwards and lifted it for him to see. The brittle shard of not-tree, that he'd limped back with. And one small leaf, unfurling skeletally from it, already blotched with decay, but determinedly growing.

Up above, the velvet darkness of the sky was giving place to a faint lambency, the most tentative of pre-dawns.

Around them, in invisible spaces beyond the walls of the world, Harry felt as though engines were shuddering into reluctant, grumbling life.

THE SKY EVENTUALLY lightened into a kind of lead-grey, glowering luminance, as though some celestial orb up there was deeply cloaked in angry cloud. The sifting not-snow became more sporadic, although it didn't stop. Out beyond the castle walls some of the trees were sprouting a kind of spidery, undirected new growth. It wasn't rebirth. It wasn't even renewal. It was something, though. A connection had been made, and Harry's feeble hands were on the crank, trying to turn it as best he could. He was prolonging matters, he suspected. He was keeping the lights on by pedalling as hard as he could, but there was a limit to how long his legs would keep going.

It gave them time.

Seitchman went travelling. Back to the real world, Harry assumed, braving the time lag, which was hopefully a bit less savage now he'd halfway got the generator going at this end. Hitting the road with Smackersnack; preparing some bolthole for fugitive monsters. Harry didn't get the chance to ask her. He found himself almost enshrined, in the heart of the castle. Swathed in rugs, clutching his stick like a sceptre, waited on by a rotating cast of miscellaneous denizens. Face screwed up in concentration as he tried to shift Underhill up a gear. To return it to life, create something new. But this had been Carolus's place for a long time, and each successive generation had been curated by the alchemist to host his migratory consciousness. Harry was a product of the bloodline gone wild, beyond Carolus's prescribed breeding program. Perhaps it was that.

Or, Harry realised bitterly, Underhill had never been built with renewal and repair in mind. It was a construct that could only ever have decayed. An inexorable expiration date that wouldn't have been important if it had fulfilled its original purpose as an incubator for Carolus's next host vessel. Horrible thought, to be that happy little Jemima having adventures with the faun and the magic dog, and then one day your lich of an ancestor appears and takes you by the hand and... scoops out your mind like an egg, because he's getting old and is ready to upgrade to the new model.

I think I can be glad we put an end to that.

HARD TO TELL how much time, given the lack of any celestial mechanics, but eventually Seitchman was back. She'd obviously been home for a change of clothes, and had a big old hiker's backpack on, sensible boots and sunglasses pushed up into her greying hair.

"Is that Dora the Explorer cosplay, or—What's going on?" Harry asked her.

He became aware that she was staring at him, and then he became aware that he'd probably looked better. The blankets he was huddled in were already crusty with mould and the skin of his hands looked greyish and blotchy.

"I've been keeping things together," he told her. "Ish."

"We need to get you out of here," she said.

"Can't," he said. "They need me. I tell them stories. It's very sad, but I'm helping."

Seitchman shrugged her pack off. "Any progress? With the whole... getting the pilot light on, turning up the heat?"

And Harry had, of course, been trying, by sheer will, by thinking in alchemical symbols, by clapping and believing in fairies. And he'd told Timon and the others, each time they asked, that, no, nothing doing, nada. And he'd been lying.

"Get them all out of here," he muttered to Seitchman. "Just you and me."

And, when she'd finally persuaded Timon and the assorted hangers on that their living battery needed some recharge time, he hunched forwards and told her the truth, at last.

"I can do it," he said. "I can feel the cogs of this place. They're all right there and ready for me to turn them. I can make a new Underhill any time I choose."

"So why haven't you?"

He studied her face. "You know, right? You've guessed?"

"I've been researching. With Smackersnack's help. She's a sharp one, once you get past all the alliteration. We've been on travels. Experimenting. A bit of alchemy of our own."

"I can recreate it all," Harry said. "But I can't *mend* it. It wasn't designed that way. It's like modelling clay, plasticine, Lego, you know? You want to make a new thing? You have to break the old thing down for materials first. I can make a new Underhill, but only if I break it all down, and *them* down. That's how Carolus did it. Wonderland on a budget. Nothing wasted. One hundred per cent recyclable."

"And so you've…"

"Held the fort. Because dumping them in the real world to live out whatever lives they'd have isn't ideal, but it's better than fucking them over like that. So maybe you've got something? Set up a nice farm upstate for them all to go live on? Free range fictional monster reservation? I mean, of the two of us, you're the smart one, right?"

Seitchman laughed. "It was your idea," she said. "Or you gave me the idea. What you said about other books, other worlds."

Harry boggled at her. "You've found another… Are we about to invade *Narnia?*"

"No, but… Look. Fairyland, right? Strange door to a magic place where everything works to wish-logic and daft rules, and sometimes there's a weird time-differential when you come out, and there are sexy maidens who lure men there, and all that."

"Your point?"

"That if *this* is real then *those* were real, or some of them. People have been stumbling onto bubble-universes like this since long before Carolus, building their little worlds, playing fairy ruler."

"And your point?"

"There are other bubbles. Alien world-building devices awaiting conscious instructions. Vacant lots for magic kingdoms. Whatever these things are. Which is a topic I intend to be the definitive expert on by the time I'm done, frankly. Though I doubt respectable journals will publish me on it."

"So you think you can just go hiking until you find one?"

"Hell, no," Seitchman said. "We found one."

HARRY WAS STUCK as Underhill's anchor for a while longer, as Smackersnack ferried the denizens out a handful at a time.

"She always knew they were there," Seitchman was explaining, sitting with him out by the web-shrouded trees around the spider's lair. "She had a whole web of connections she made, as she hunted for a way out. She found our world, obviously. But she found other places, too. Only she didn't know what they were. They were just... dead space. They didn't react to her. I guess she's too low energy to trigger them, or they just register her as something *made*. There's that whole fairytale thing of fairies being as good as or better than mortals in every respect except they don't have souls, isn't there? After chatting with you, I got to chatting with her, and she took me there. I felt it react. To me. Like Carolus must once have done, coming here. A tabula rasa world."

She'd taken a census of Underhill, surveyed the Odlins and the fauns and the miscellaneous creatures. Asked them what they wanted, in a new home. Mod cons for a magic kingdom under construction.

Getting Gombles across had been challenging. Harry had almost asked if they *had* to save the thing, but that was unworthy of him, he knew. Seitchman's watchword was *No clown left behind*. And so even Gombles had been bundled through to his final reward in the new land of opportunity. Harry didn't even want to imagine what that meant.

"And then what?" he asked Seitchman. "When you've got everything set up for them. I mean, these places aren't indefinitely self-sustaining, are they? That was Carolus's whole problem. The energy economy."

"It's an odd thing, about all the stories," Seitchman remarked. "Find a magic world. Have magical adventures. Back in time for tea."

"And you have been back. Back home."

"In time for various meals, at random intervals. Dealing with my email backlog and journal deadlines. And passing on your regards. Explaining how you're *seriously* self-isolating."

"It's still on, then?"

"Looks like it's starting to come to an end, but the whole vaccination thing's dragging out, as per usual. But people haven't declared you legally dead, and hopefully you can pick up some sort of career when you finally, you know…"

"You're dodging my original question," he noted. Smackersnack bustled by with a couple of Odlins, ready for another trip.

"It always annoyed me," Seitchman continued to dodge. "The way those stories had to end with the primacy of the real world. I had, I'll admit, a fairly shitty childhood. Show me a portal to fairyland, you'd not have seen me for dust. But always it's back in time for tea, because God forbid the magic can last."

"But the magic can't last," Harry pointed out reasonably. "That's the point. I mean, I get it. You don't intend to go back. But time will still catch up with you like it did with Carolus. And we saw how *he* ended up solving the problem."

"Maybe when it's used up, we find a new bubble," Seitchman said. "Maybe I recruit an heir who'll take over when I'm too old and the lights start going out. And I don't mean the way Carolus did. I mean finding someone to take over from me, not for me to take over. Or maybe there should be a trust. I mean, hereditary monarchy or just serial autocracy, it's still a bit of a crap system. I think I can set up a mechanism for a peaceful transition of management. Perhaps I can suborn the bloody Underlings, even. But this way I've got a few decades to find my feet and get things going."

"I always used to hate that too," Harry admitted slowly. "That you had to go home. Or worse, you woke up and it was all a dream and the magic hadn't even been real."

"And?" Seitchman asked carefully.

"And now I've grown up and put away childish things and I really want the internet and hot water and takeaways and things. And flush toilets. You wouldn't think you'd miss flush toilets when you're stuck somewhere you don't even have to poop, but apparently you can. I want to go home and pick up where I left off."

Seitchman nodded. "Well, that's convenient, because it means *you* can start delivering *my* correspondence instead of the other way round."

A hand fell on Harry's shoulder: Timon crouched next to them.

"It's our turn," he said. "Hulder and Wish Dog and me. We're the last. So, you know, goodbyes and all."

* * *

AND, AFTER THEY'D gone, the cold. The insistent powdering of fresh non-snow that was the basic fabric of Underhill reducing to its dead state. And Harry felt he could let go and let it all start to decay again. Let the sky go out and the brief blooms of decay accelerate towards total dissolution. *Or should we even have saved the fungus?* Except it wasn't even real fungus, just the process of the unreal degrading into the non-existent, as seen through a deranged alchemist's imagination.

He'd decided what he was going to do with his life, by then.

Smackersnack came back that one last time, and asked if he was still sure. But yes. Home in time for tea. Home to a familiar world where he could, if he was so inclined, pretend it had all been his overwrought imagination. Turn his back on the magic. Except that wasn't quite the plan.

Perhaps the most remarkable part of the whole business was that he still had his house keys. Also, despite being two months in arrears of rent, no new tenant had arrived to bin his stuff and sleep in his bed. Possibly the national emergency had been good for something. He started charging his phone and making calls.

"You want to do what now?" his agent demanded. Not as incredulous as Harry had expected, though. Almost intrigued.

"I think it's about time for a new adaptation," Harry confirmed. "I can't even remember where the rights are these days, even. Did they revert to me? Are they public? Does that German film company still have them?"

"No idea, mate, but I'll look it out. And even if someone is still sitting on them, doesn't mean we can't get them back or work with them, or… I mean, having you attached to the project, that's going to count for something, right?" Sounding more enthusiastic about Harry's career than he had in a while.

"And new books," Harry decided. "Update the franchise."

"Can you even write a book?" his agent asked doubtfully.

"We'll find out. Or I'll find someone who can and work with them." *And I'll not want for new material*, he thought. *Although I don't think I'll be able to credit my sources.* "Underhill is going to be a *thing*, Steve. I'll make it one. We're going to make *money*." Because he'd have need of money, maybe. He might want to buy some out of the way place where a lot of strange friends could come and crash if they needed to.

"Actual money? Fancy that," his agent said philosophically. "Well, who knows? Weirder things have happened."

Harry glanced over to Timon, who was hunched on the sofa, balancing a coffee mug and a little cake on a saucer. "They have," he agreed fiercely. "They really have."

ACKNOWLEDGEMENTS

Thank you to my beta readers and fact checkers
Liz Myles, Emma Reeves and Chantal Delaney
for keeping me on the straight and narrow
with various parts of this narrative.

FIND US ONLINE!

www.rebellionpublishing.com

/rebellionpub   /rebellionpublishing /rebellionpublishing

SIGN UP TO OUR NEWSLETTER!

rebellionpublishing.com/newsletter

YOUR REVIEWS MATTER!

Enjoy this book? Got something to say?

Leave a review on Amazon, GoodReads or with your favourite bookseller and let the world know!